5-MINUTE MARVEL STORIES

MARVEL

Los Angeles
New York

"The New Spider-Man in Town" written by Andy Schmidt.
Illustrated by Aurelio Mazzara and Gaetano Petrigno.

"A Family Affair" written by Colin Hosten. Illustrated by Georges Duarte.

"Journey to Justice" written by Andy Schmidt. Illustrated by Eduardo Mello.

"Attack of the Portal Crashers" written by Calliope Glass. Illustrated by Aurelio Mazzara
and Gaetano Petrigno.

"The Switch Up" written by Brandon T. Snider. Illustrated by Eduardo Mello.

"Full Force!" written by Alexandra West and Calliope Glass. Illustrated by
Cucca Vincenzo and Salvatore Di Marco.

"Rocket Science" written by Brandon T. Snider. Illustrated by Simone Buonfantino.

"Island of the Cyborgs" written by Ray Caban. Illustrated by Eduardo Mello.

"Iron Man: Invincible!" written by Andy Schmidt. Illustrated by Dario Brizuela and
Gaetano Petrigno.

"The Hunt for Black Panther" written by Jordan Lurie. Illustrated by Aurelio Mazzara
and Gaetano Petrigno.

"Mixed Signals from Knowhere" written by Colin Hosten. Illustrated by Aurelio Mazzara
and Gaetano Petrigno.

"Ultron Goes Viral" written by Calliope Glass. Illustrated by Cucca Vincenzo and
Salvatore Di Marco.

All stories painted by Anna Beliashova, Vita Efremova,
Tommaso Moscardin, Ekaterina Myshalova, and Jay David Ramos.

Storybook designed by David Roe

Cover illustrated by Eduardo Mello
Cover painted by Vita Efremova

All based upon Marvel Comics' characters and stories.

For information address Marvel Press, 125 West End Avenue, New York, New York 10023.

Printed in the United States of America

First Edition, April 2019

Library of Congress Control Number: 2018952319

10 9 8 7 6 5 4 3 2

ISBN: 978-1-368-02667-3

FAC-038091-19253

Visit www.MarvelHQ.com

MARVEL
©2019 MARVEL

CONTENTS

The New Spider-Man in Town   1

A Family Affair   17

Journey to Justice   33

Attack of the Portal Crashers   47

The Switch Up   63

Full Force!   81

Rocket Science   95

Island of the Cyborgs   111

Iron Man: Invincible!   127

The Hunt for Black Panther   141

Mixed Signals from Knowhere   157

Ultron Goes Viral   173

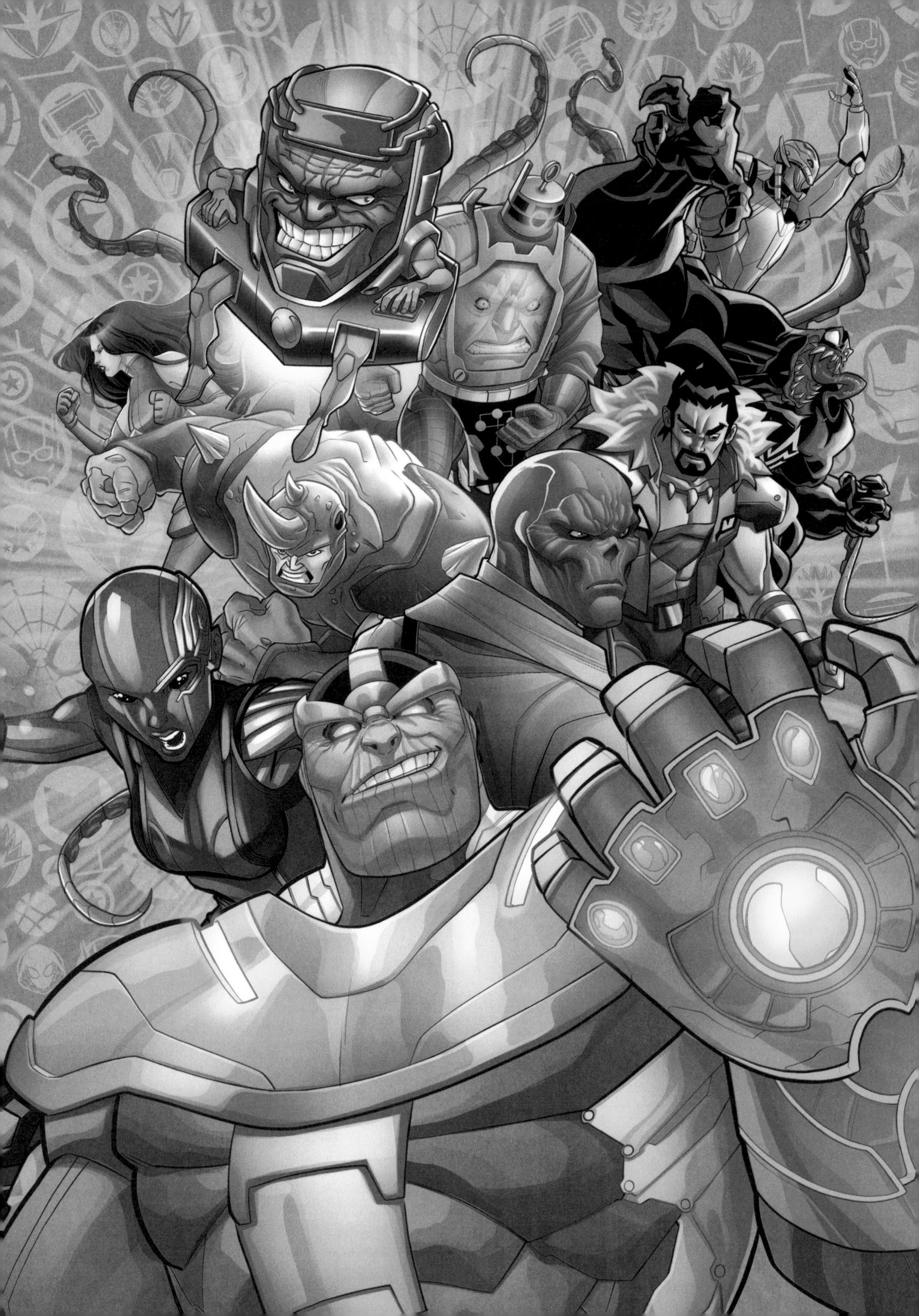

The New Spider-Man in Town

Miles Morales is a student at Midtown High School in New York City. He's happy and he has a thirst for knowledge—especially science. He was a young boy just like any other, working hard and doing the right thing, but something soon happened that changed his life for good. . . .

While in chemistry class, Miles noticed that his good friend—
Peter Parker—kept sneaking out of school. Miles grew suspicious,
wondering if something was wrong with Peter—if he was okay.

So one day, Miles followed Peter and watched as he snuck a
mask from his bag. But it wasn't just any mask that Peter was
sneaking—it was Spider-Man's mask!

Miles couldn't believe it. When Peter was leaving school that
afternoon, Miles called to Peter, "Hey, Peter, where are you
headed?"

Peter awkwardly smiled back and said, "Uh, I've got an assignment
for the *Daily Bugle* . . . uh . . . Yeah . . . I've . . . I've got to go!"
Miles didn't believe that either. He followed Peter to a giant lab.

Inside the lab, Miles lost track of Peter, and he didn't notice the genetically altered spider slowly spinning a web and dropping down toward him.

"YEE-OW!" The spider bit Miles right on the hand! Miles knocked it off. He knew instantly that this was no ordinary spider bite.

Instead of getting sick from the spider bite, Miles soon discovered that it gave him spider-powers. "I've got to figure out what this means! What should I do?" He ran home fast.

"Think! Think! Think," Miles told himself. "If Peter really is Spider-Man, then what did he do?" Miles searched for articles about Spider-Man. "Okay, so you get powers. Check. Then what? You make a costume and go stop bad guys. That seems obvious!"

With that, Miles created his own Spider-Man costume and leapt into the city.

"I can run on walls," Miles yelled as he scaled the side of a building! He was enjoying discovering his powers, and climbing walls wasn't the only one! Miles soon discovered he had an amazing spider-sense that warned him of danger.

"What the heck?" Miles couldn't ignore the ringing in his brain. That's when he noticed the burglars running behind him. In that instant, what started off as fun became very scary.

Miles had a really big decision to make. Should he run from the danger and stay safe, or should he use his new powers to try to stop these villains?

Miles realized that if he was going to call himself Spider-Man, he was going to have to act like Spider-Man!

Much to his surprise, Peter Parker—as the original Spider-Man—was already on the case! One of the criminals was getting away, but Miles was able to help. "Hold on helmet head," he announced. "The only place you're racing off to is prison!" Miles had powers to match Peter's and was easily able to contain the thief.

It wasn't until the action was over that Miles realized just how much danger he was really in. He climbed to the top of a building and wanted to fade away—which is exactly what he did: This was a brand-new power, one that Peter didn't have! He camouflaged himself into his surroundings.

Peter Parker swung up to where Miles had been. "Miles, is that you?" Peter called out. "I recognized your voice. Believe it or not, I know what you're thinking. I went through the same thing when I first got my powers."

Miles was stunned. "You did?"

"Sure, I did," Peter said. "My uncle Ben used to tell me that with great power, there must also come great responsibility."

Peter tossed Miles something from his costume. "Here, you can have these extra web-shooters for now," said Peter.

"Whoa! Cool!" Miles said while testing out the web-shooters.

Miles looked up to Peter, figuring out what he should do. "Maybe I can follow you around for a few days. You know, see how it goes?"

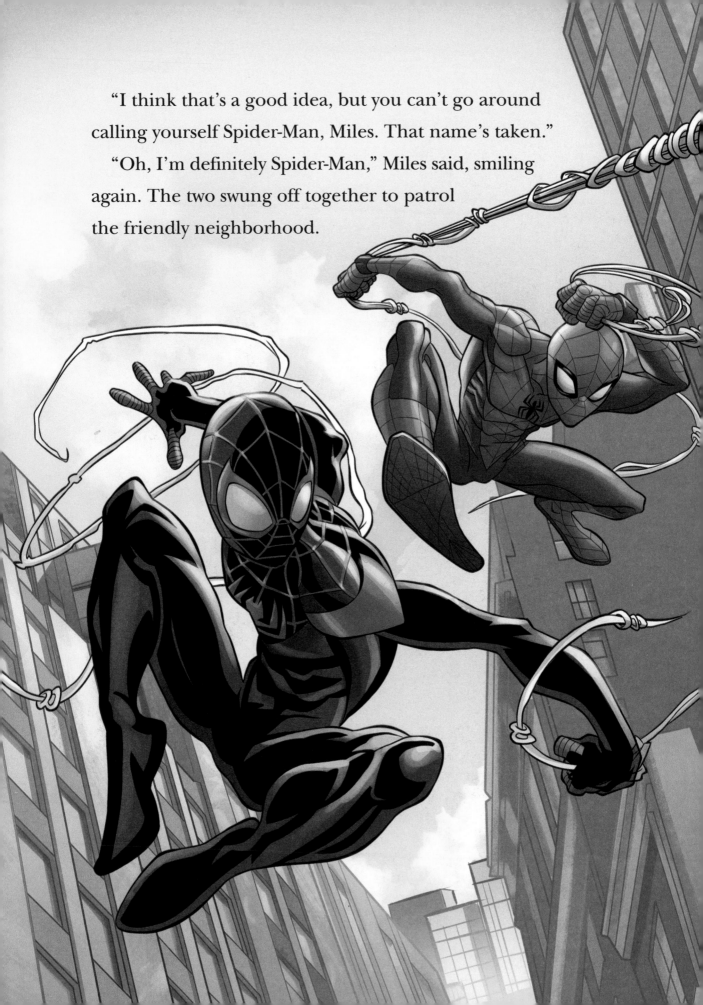

"I think that's a good idea, but you can't go around calling yourself Spider-Man, Miles. That name's taken."

"Oh, I'm definitely Spider-Man," Miles said, smiling again. The two swung off together to patrol the friendly neighborhood.

It wasn't long before Peter
got them into quite a pickle—
surrounded by some of the
nastiest villains in New York City!
And that's when Miles knew . . .

. . . he was born for this!

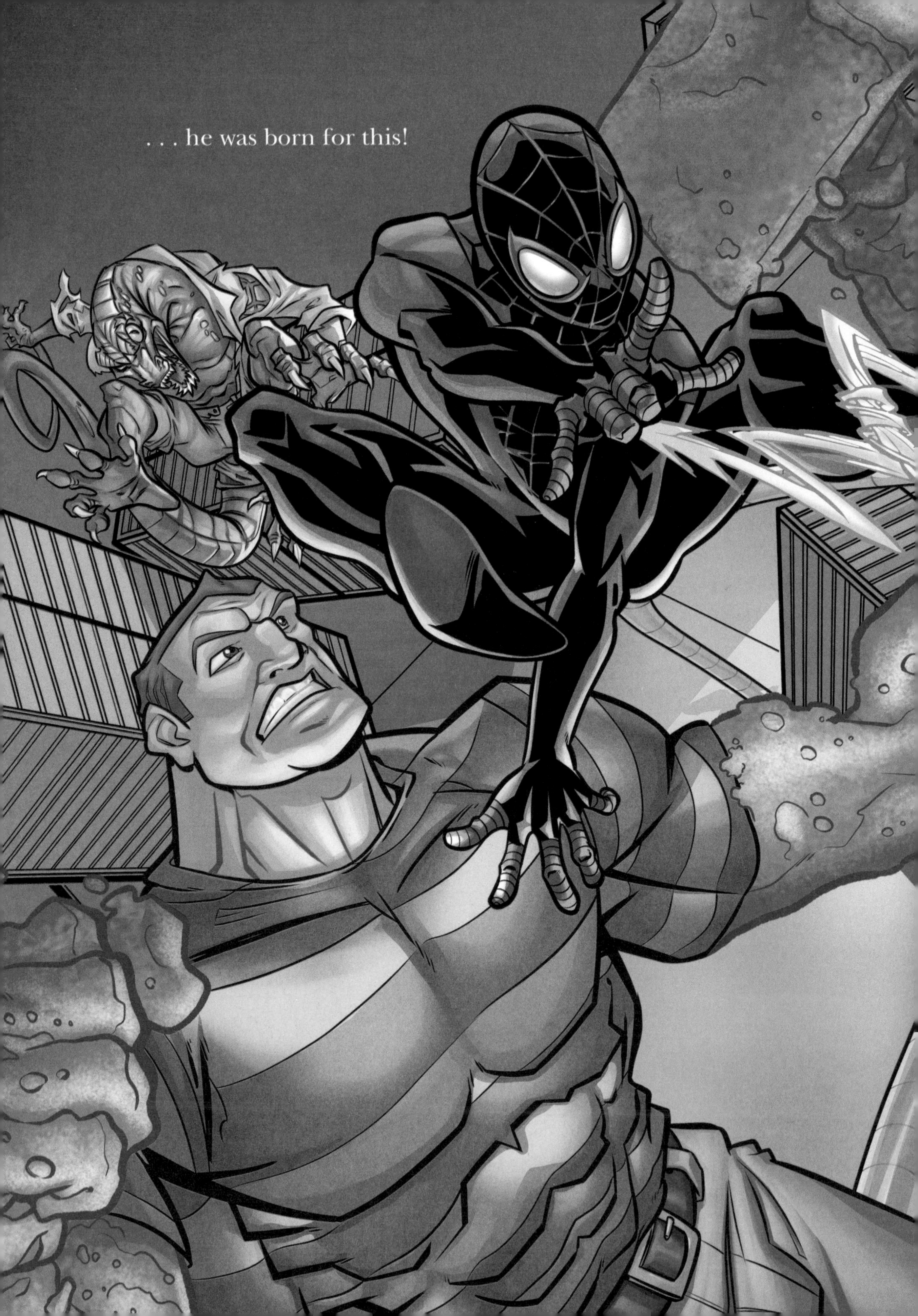

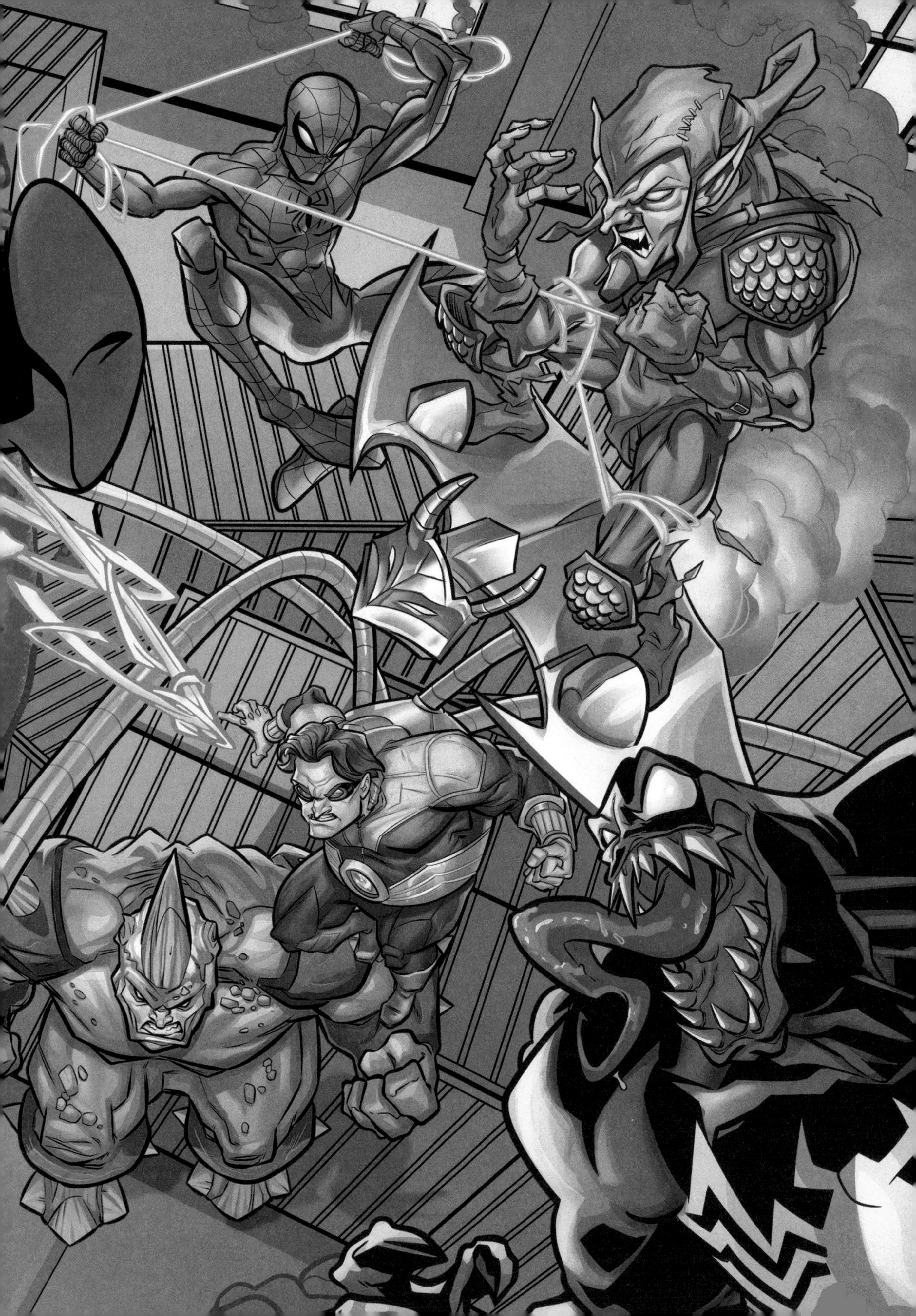

The battle roared while Peter kept poking fun at the rampaging villains. Miles was terrified. "How do you keep joking in the middle of a fight?" he asked Peter. "Aren't you scared?" That's when the Rhino grabbed Peter by the neck. Peter couldn't let out another word—funny or otherwise!

Miles turned and let loose his newest and last power— another power that Peter didn't have at all. Miles would later call it his venom strike! And it put Rhino down for the count! Peter was safe!

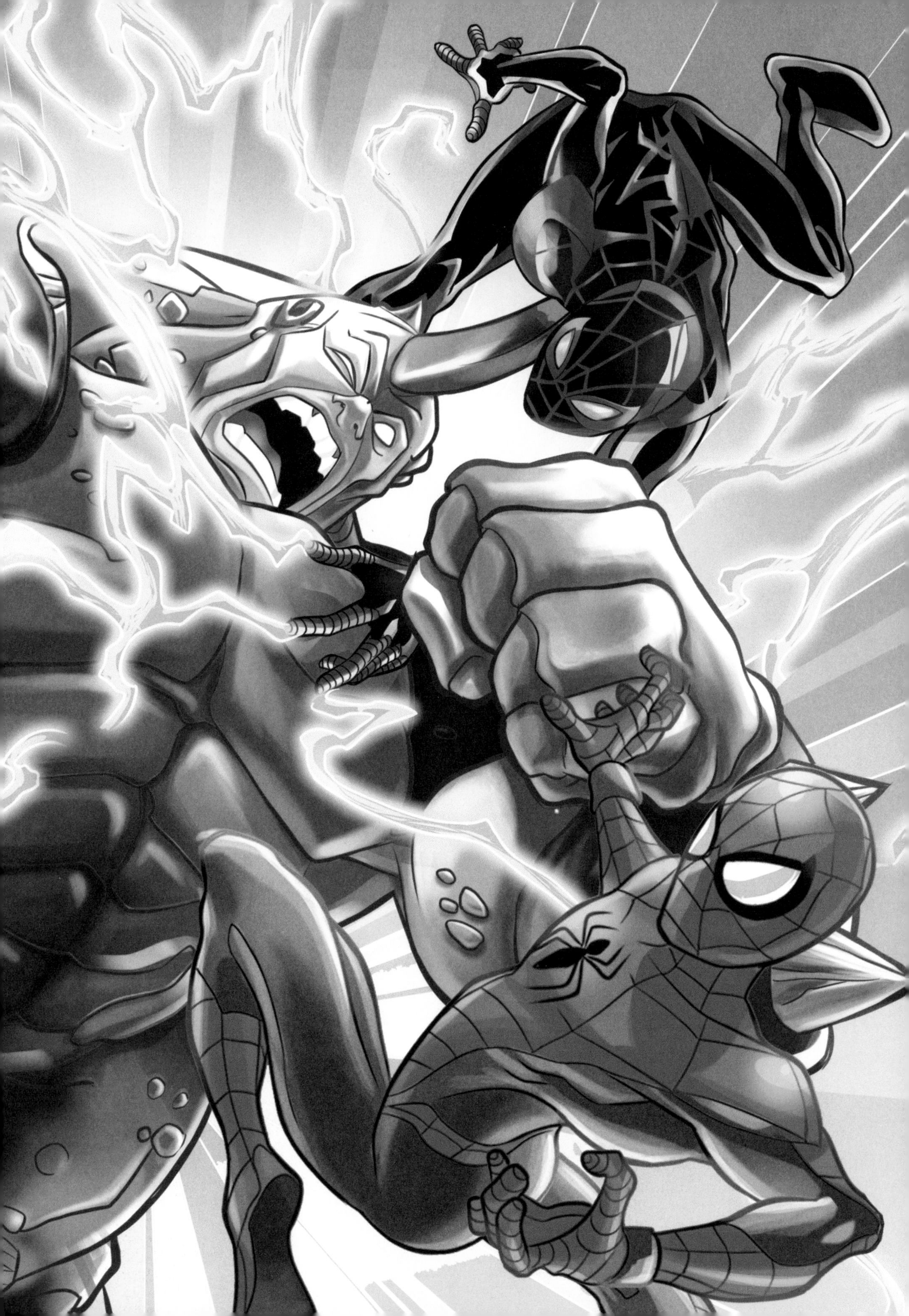

Miles and Peter wrapped the baddies up in maybe a little more than the usual amount of sticky stuff. Peter said, "Come on, if you're not going to change your name, you've got to learn how to crack jokes—it's part of the job. Give it a try."

Miles scratched his head, thinking while looking down at the webbed-up villains. Then he said, "Looks like you've got yourselves into a sticky situation, uh, evil-doers."

Peter sighed. "Wow. Somebody call the doctor—you have no funny bone."

A Family Affair

On a quiet night in the galaxy, the Guardians were gathered in the *Milano*, waiting for their next big mission.

Just then, the ship's incoming message light began to blink. The Guardians all huddled over the light.

"Oh boy," Rocket said. "Nebula has stolen a device from Nova Corps, and they need our help!"

Gamora was thinking about her adoptive sister, Nebula. She couldn't help but think about their history and the sibling rivalry that started early in their lives. As young girls, Gamora and Nebula had been taken in by the most feared Super Villain in the universe: Thanos!

Thanos had been a harsh parent to Gamora and Nebula. To inspire competition between the two, he forced them to fight each other over and over again.

Gamora ran away from her evil family in search of something better. She joined Star-Lord on his adventures, but she often wished Nebula would have joined them, too.

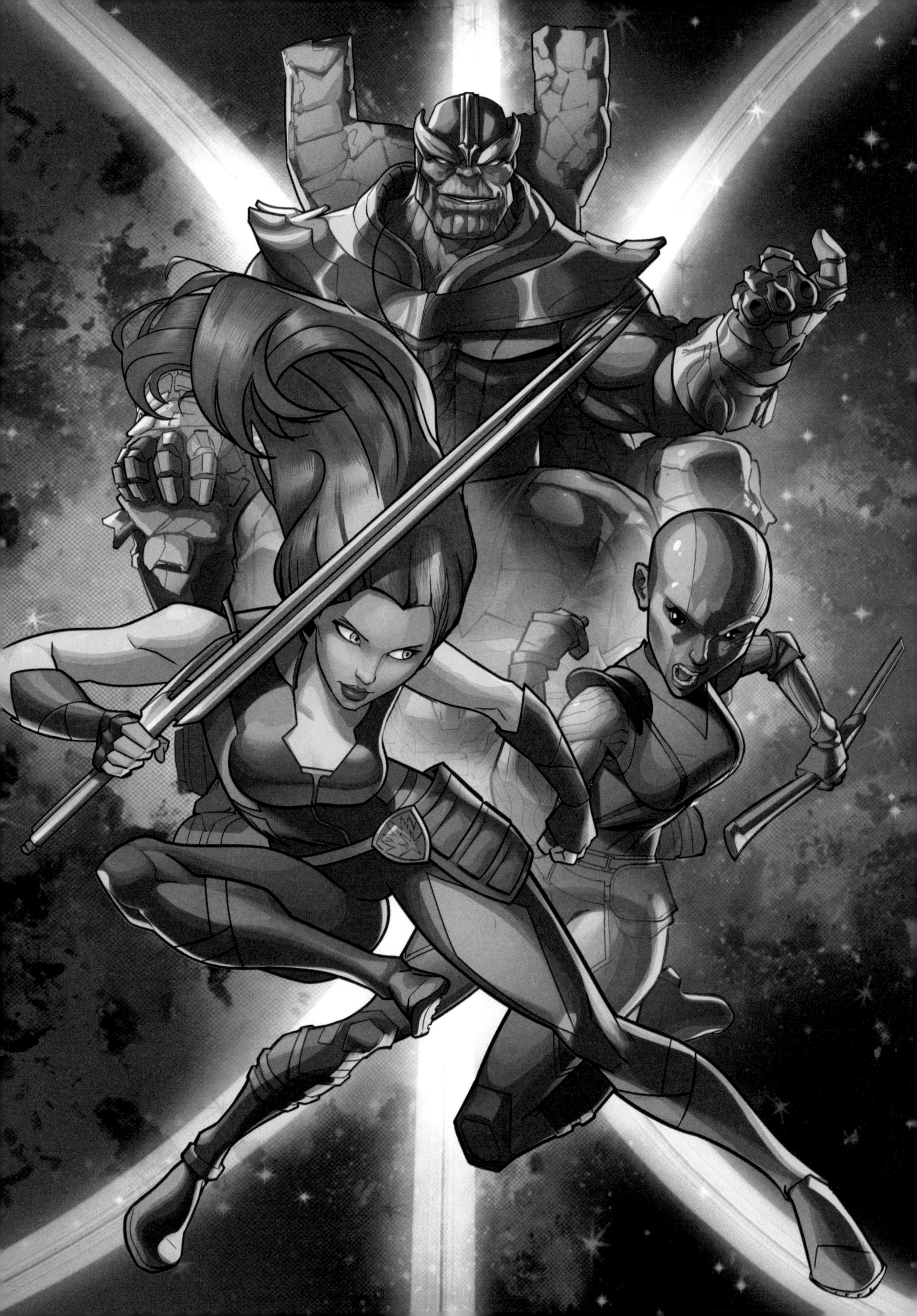

The Guardians sprang into action. Gamora guided Rocket and Star-Lord as they flew the *Milano*, chasing after Nebula. Gamora knew she couldn't let Nebula get away. They flew through the galaxy, following Gamora's lead. They landed on Morag, and Star-Lord was skeptical. But Gamora had a feeling.

"If this is where you're hiding," Gamora muttered as they landed, "then I'll find you."

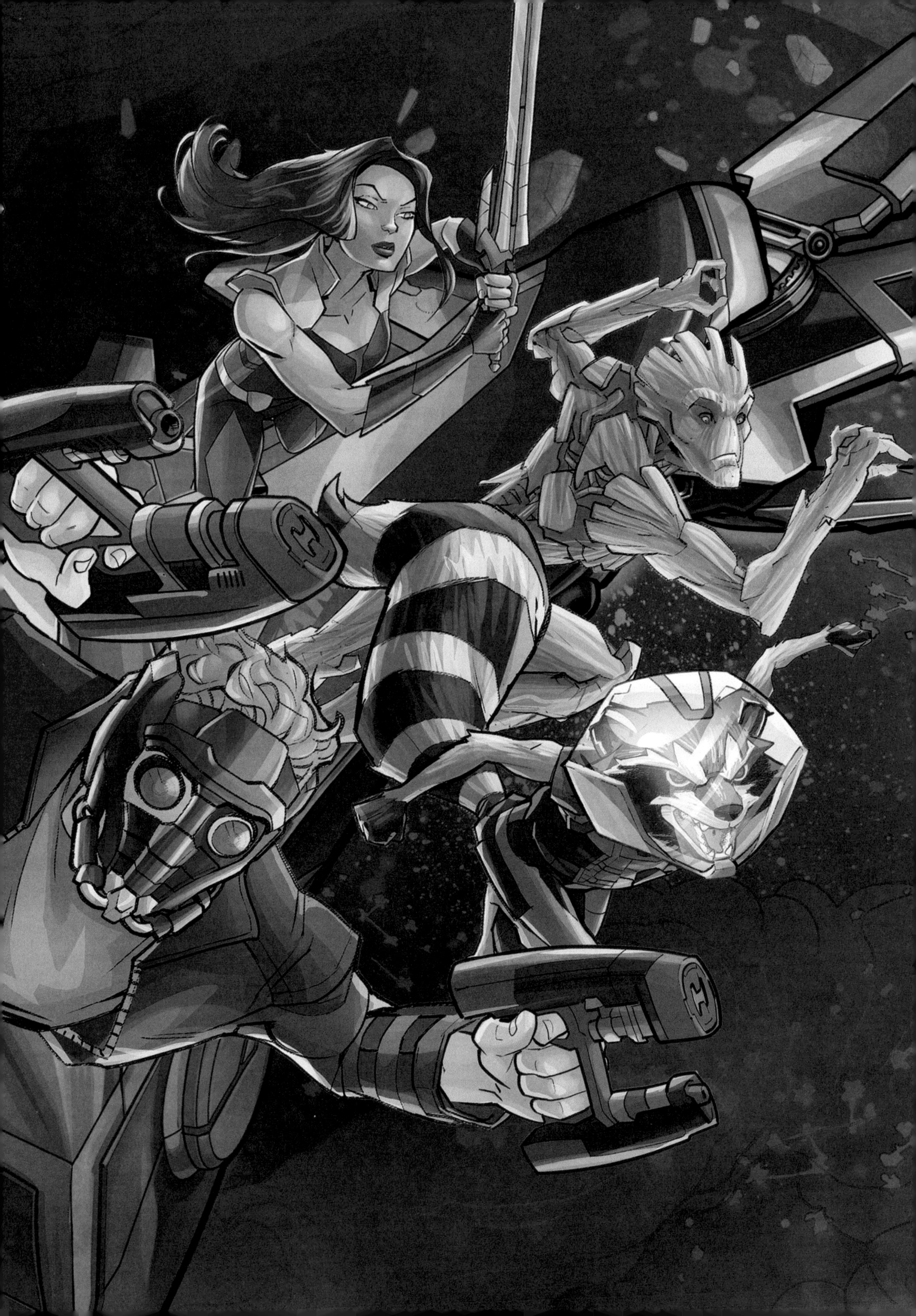

She'd caught Nebula stealing in the past, and had learned that she was wired into a whole underground network for black-market goods, linked by the subterranean tunnels of Morag. Gamora ran ahead of the rest of the Guardians. She navigated the streets until she spotted an old wooden door with strange markings etched into it. She descended a creaky staircase into the darkness below.

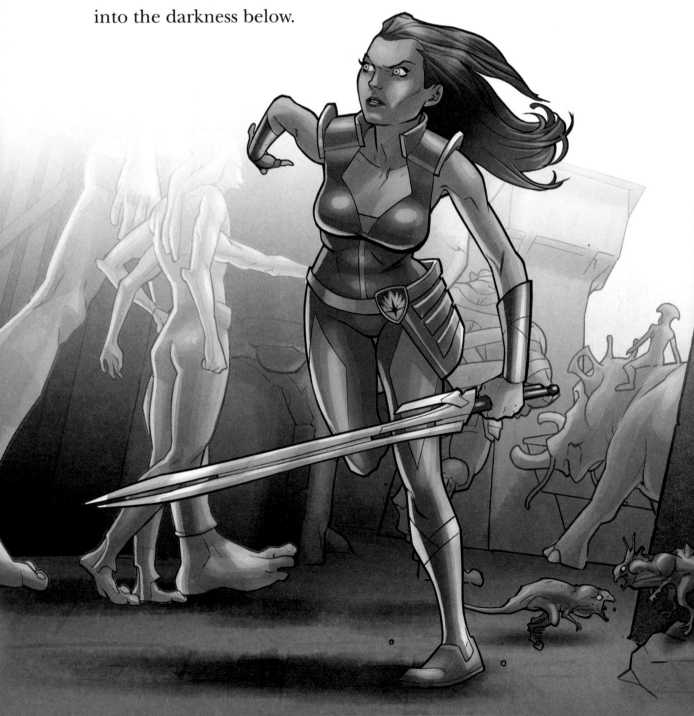

Soon Gamora heard a low voice in the distance. Up ahead, she saw a shaft of light where the tunnel ended, leading into a large room. She slowly crept toward the entrance.

"Is someone there?" Nebula's voice rang out. "Why don't you quit skulking in the shadows and reveal yourself?"

Busted. Gamora entered the room to find Nebula standing in a corner holding a strange-looking device. It was round and covered with dials and buttons. Gamora thought it must be some kind of weapon.

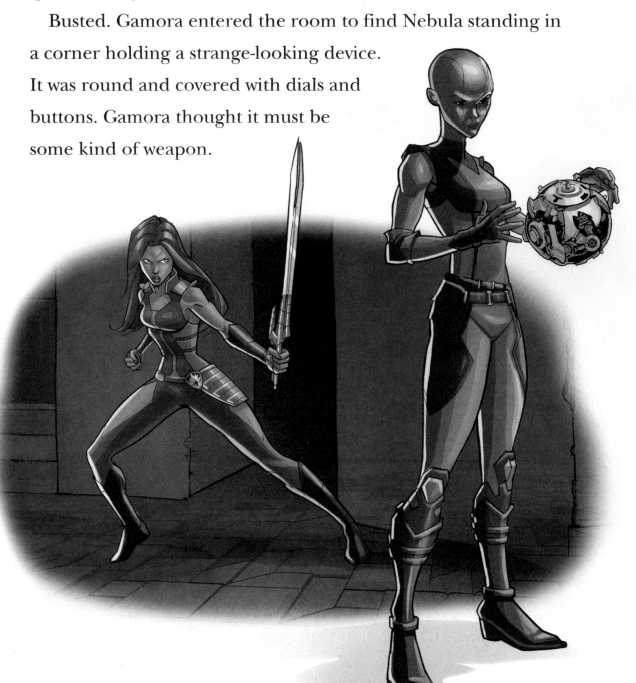

"Ah, Gamora," Nebula said, "what a very unpleasant surprise!"
Gamora rolled her eyes. "Time's up, sister of mine," she
snarled as she lunged at Nebula. But Nebula pressed a button on
the device she was holding, and Gamora froze.

In horror, Gamora watched her arm lower itself and drop her sword. Gamora was powerless to respond. Nebula seemed to be controlling her body with the device!

"Clever, isn't it?" Nebula said. "They're doing all sorts of wonderful things with technology at Nova Corps these days. Imagine all the trouble I can cause now!"

Suddenly Star-Lord burst into the room. "Not so fast! When you mess with Gamora, you mess with all of us!"

Rocket ran in behind Star-Lord, holding a giant cannon. Then Drax came in. He looked over at Gamora and said, "Why is she just standing there?"

"I am Groot?" a deep voice boomed out. Groot lumbered through the doorway.

"No, pal," Rocket said. "I don't think she turned into a tree."

"Okay," Star-Lord said to Nebula, "we can do this the easy way, or the fun way."

Nebula grinned. "Let's have some fun, shall we?"

Just then, Nebula pressed a button on the device and thrust it in the Guardians' direction. The whole team froze where they were. Nebula turned her back to the Guardians, and because she was distracted, Rocket managed to free his hand. He shot his cannon, destroying the Nova Corps device.

When the device shattered, the Guardians were released from Nebula's hold. The Guardians flexed their limbs as they regained control of their bodies.

Gamora picked up her sword and turned to face Nebula. But her sister was already on the move.

The Guardians followed Nebula into the tunnels. Gamora was the first to catch up with her sister.

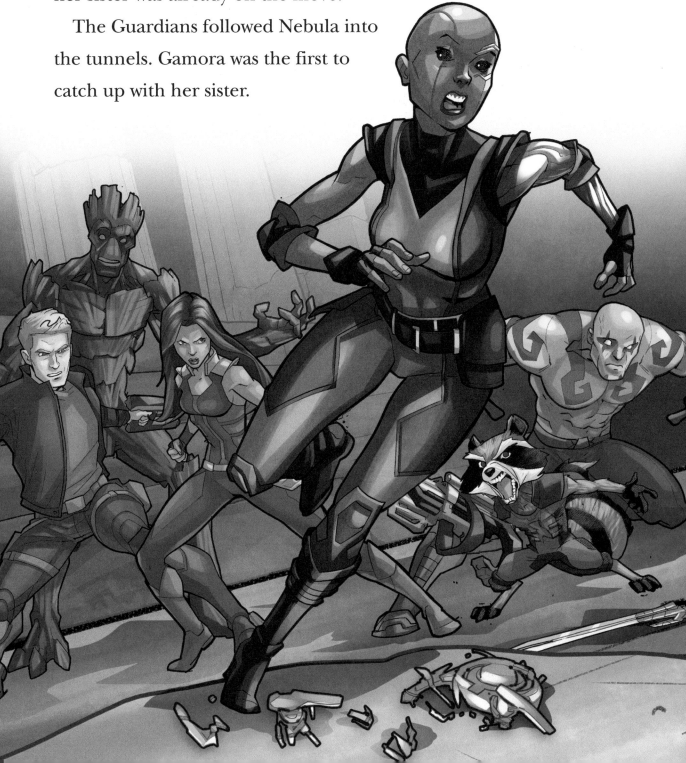

"You want us to hang back while you take her?" Star-Lord asked Gamora as the Guardians caught up.

Gamora had learned that family didn't just mean being raised together, but being there for each other.

Her real family was standing right in front of her. And she needed their help to defeat her adopted sister.

She shook her head. "No," she said. "We're a team—let's do this together."

The team nodded at Gamora as they headed toward Nebula. With some help from Drax and the rest of the team, Gamora propelled toward Nebula and knocked her off her feet.

The Guardians watched as Gamora handcuffed Nebula. "Now you're the one who can't move, sister," she said smugly.

Gamora turned to the Guardians. "You know, we're not just a team. You guys are also my family."

"I am Groot," Groot said proudly.

Rocket muttered, "You're right—this is one weird, dysfunctional family!"

Gamora laughed. "I wouldn't have it any other way."

MARVEL
Journey to Justice

As war broke out across the world in the 1940s, ruthless forces such as Hydra, directed by the villainous Red Skull, Arnim Zola, and Baron Zemo tore through Europe. The world was in need of a hero—someone to stand up and fight for all people—and no one would have ever guessed who that hero would be. . . .

In the borough of Brooklyn in the great city of New York, Steve Rogers sat, dismayed by the newsreels he watched in his local theater.

"Every week the news gets worse," Steve said to himself. "I can't let my friends fight these battles alone." He had to help stop the growing tide of evil!

Though he was small and suffered from asthma, Steve Rogers desperately wanted to help fight for what was right.

"Sorry, kid," the recruitment officer said, "there's nothing I can do—NEXT!" The army saw only Steve's size and illness. But that wouldn't stop Steve Rogers.

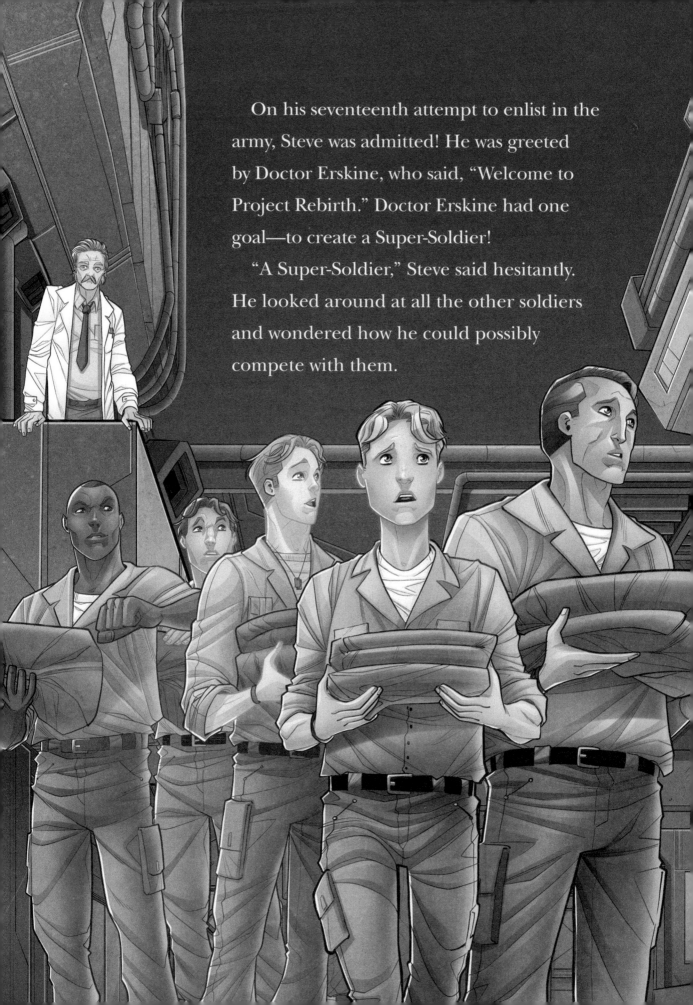

On his seventeenth attempt to enlist in the army, Steve was admitted! He was greeted by Doctor Erskine, who said, "Welcome to Project Rebirth." Doctor Erskine had one goal—to create a Super-Soldier!

"A Super-Soldier," Steve said hesitantly. He looked around at all the other soldiers and wondered how he could possibly compete with them.

When all the soldiers were sent on long runs, Steve was always in last place. They did weight training, and Steve could barely heft the lightest dumbbells.

When the time came to choose their first candidate to undergo the Super-Soldier protocols, it was Steve Rogers who was chosen by Doctor Erskine. "You never give up, Steve. You believe deeply in fighting for freedom and protecting those who can't protect themselves," said Erskine. "That is why I have chosen you."

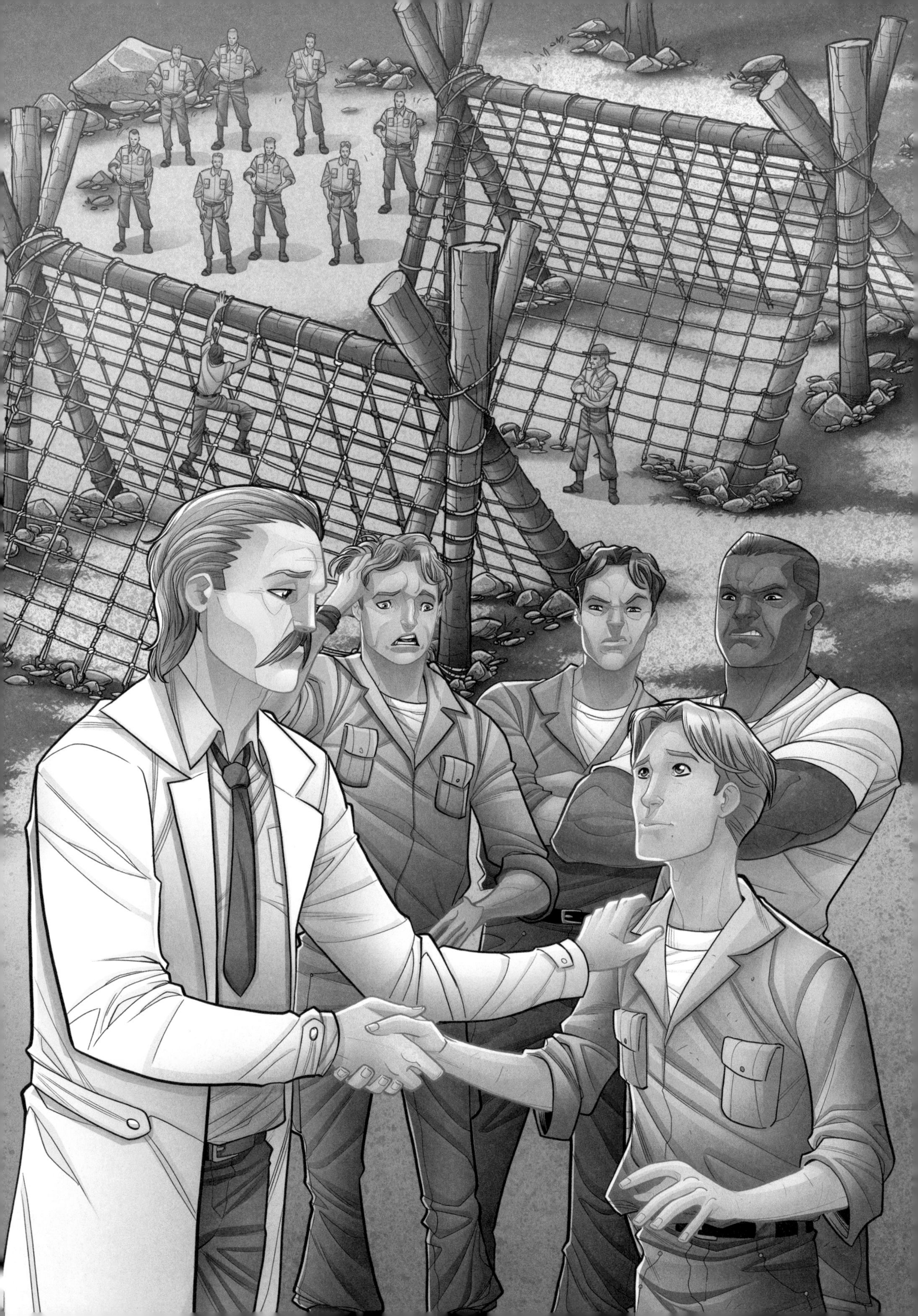

Steve stared at the Super-Soldier Serum he was supposed to drink.

"Don't worry, Steve," Doctor Erskine said. "After your transformation, you'll know it was worth it." Steve drank the secret formula and was bombarded with Vita Rays.

Within seconds, the transformation was complete, and where a ninety-eight-pound weakling once stood, now towered the world's first Super-Soldier! Captain America was born!

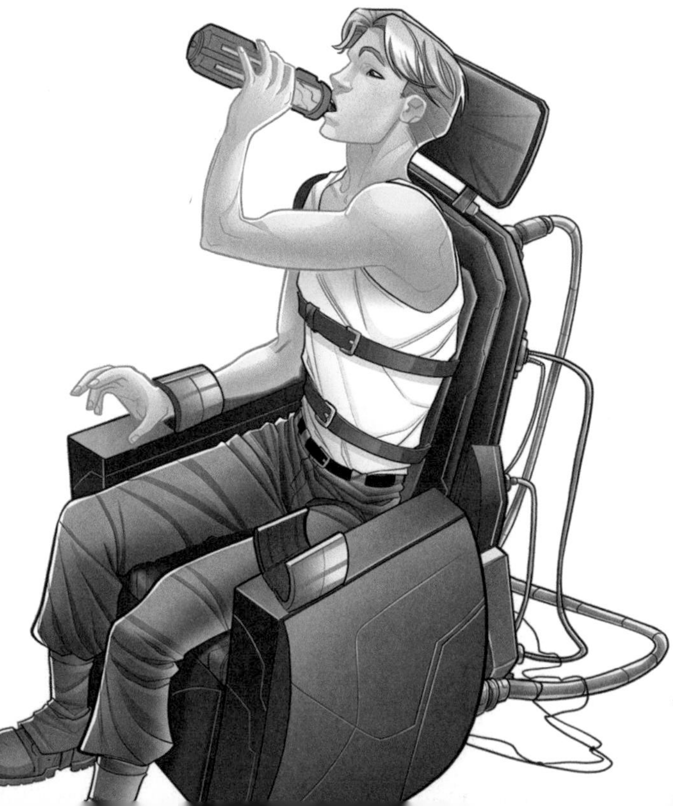

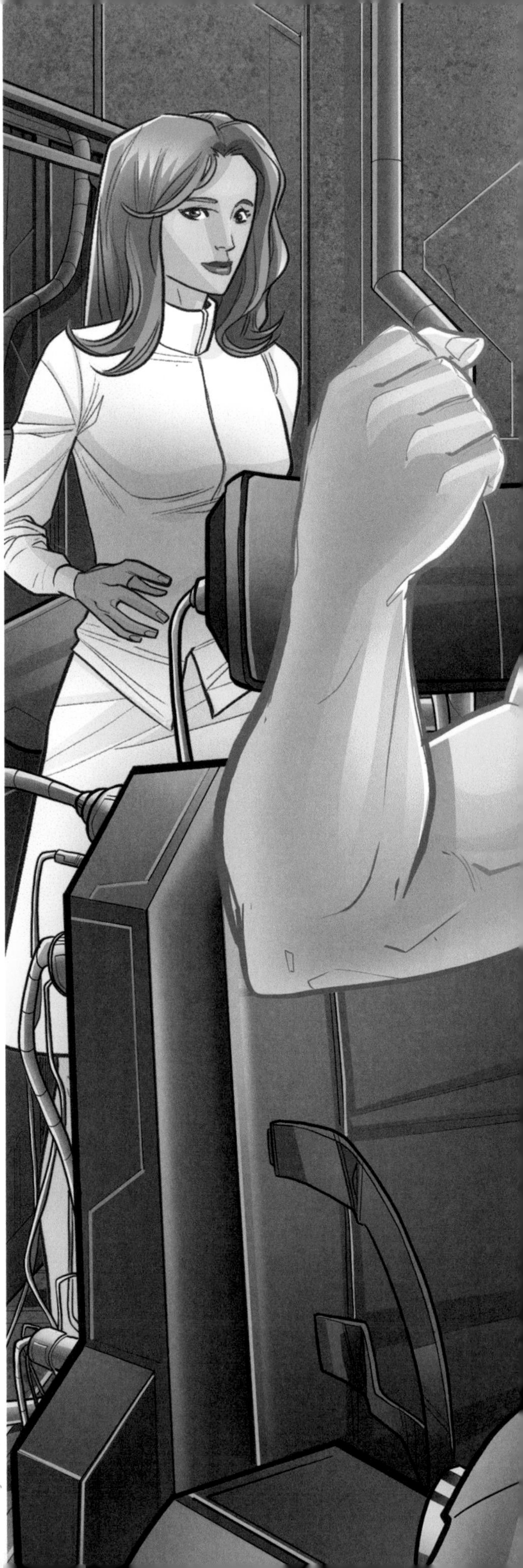

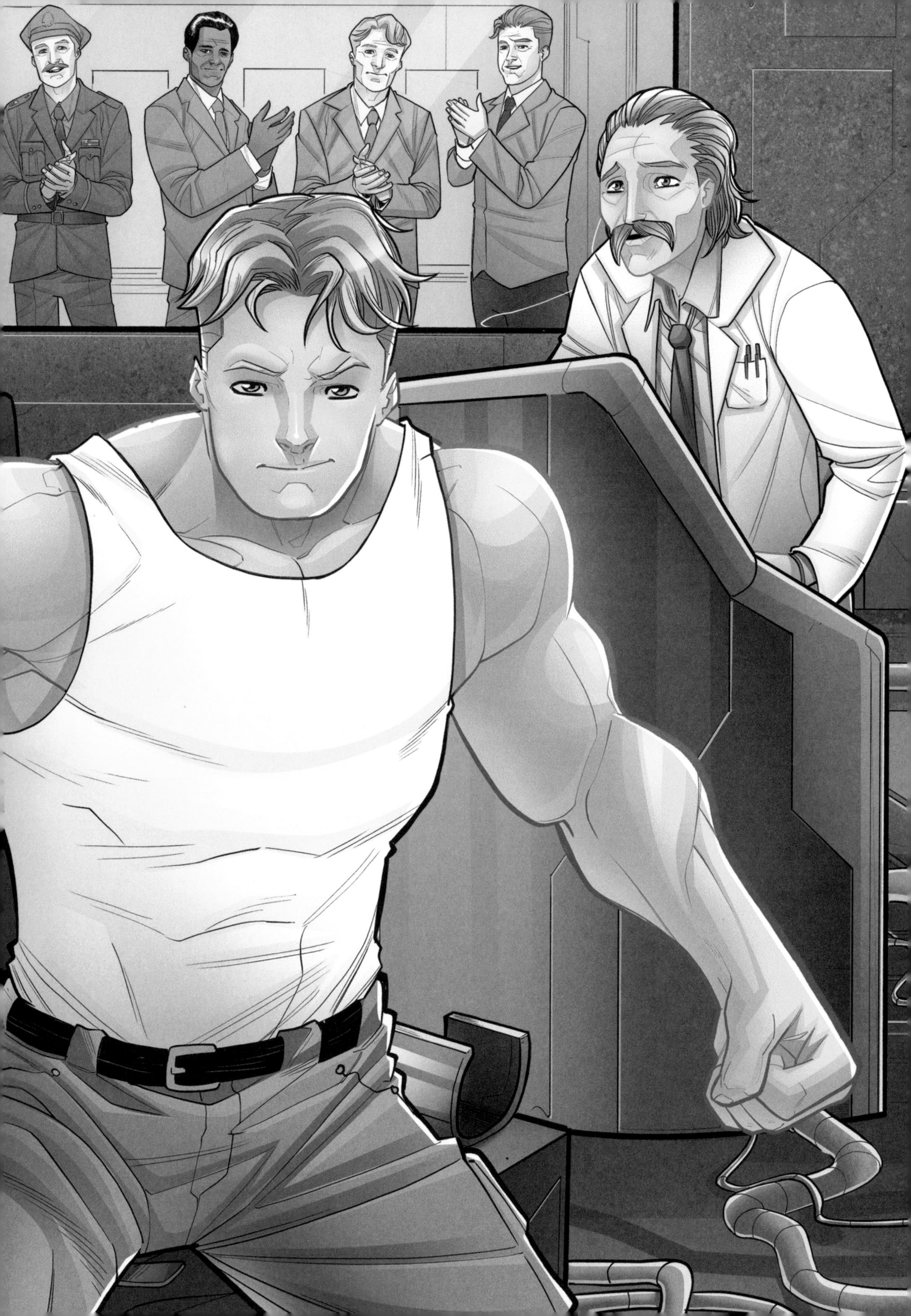

Steve wasted no time, getting straight to work, fighting for freedom across the globe! He helped to turn the tide of the war and beat back the evil forces running wild!

"You soldiers have braved the front lines," Captain America told the troops. "Today I fight with you, and we will honor our country and our cause. For freedom!"

Captain America was joined by Bucky Barnes, his trusty sidekick. Bucky was the bouncy, happy-go-lucky one of the two, but that didn't mean they weren't the two bravest soldiers in the world. Together, they would fight villains like the Red Skull and Arnim Zola—and take them down!

By the end of the war, only Baron Zemo remained to be captured. Captain America and Bucky charged into Zemo's family castle. "Watch out for booby traps, Bucky," Cap shouted. And the duo dodged every one of them. But Zemo would not be stopped so easily.

"Captain, you have foiled all of my plans except one," Baron Zemo taunted.

Even as Captain America tied Baron Zemo up, Zemo set his
final attack into motion. "My rocket is loaded and aimed at New
York! And you can't stop it!"

Zemo's rocket took off. The rumble was deafening. "Oh, no,"
Steve said. "It's aimed at my home!"

Thinking fast, Steve jumped onto the rocket, taking him far into the sky and way out to sea. He broke into the rocket's guidance system, causing it to fall harmlessly into the freezing ocean below.

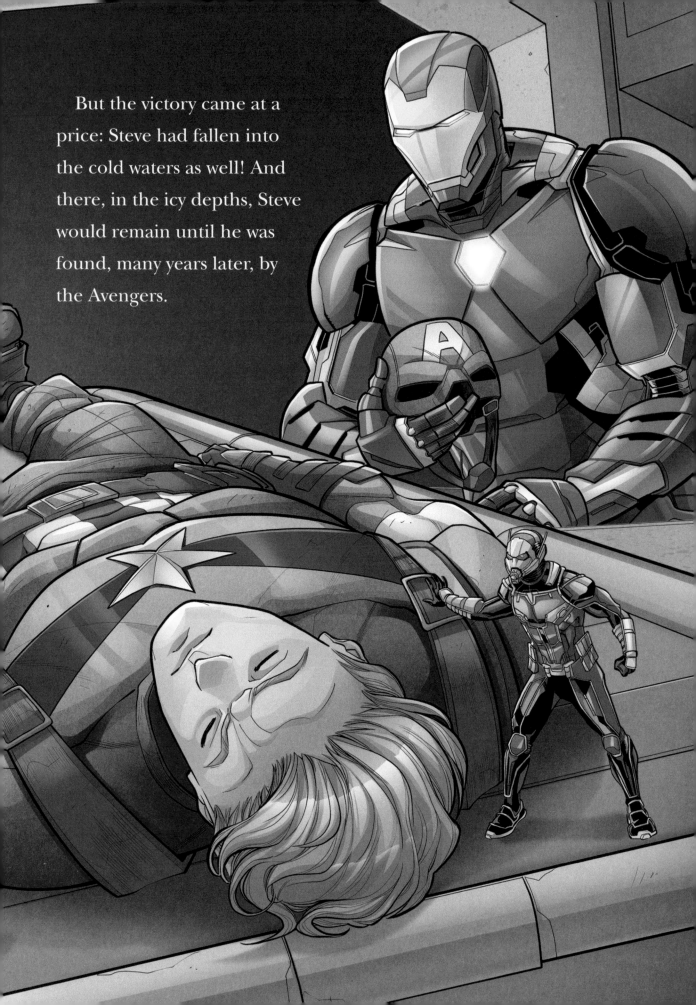

But the victory came at a price: Steve had fallen into the cold waters as well! And there, in the icy depths, Steve would remain until he was found, many years later, by the Avengers.

Now, Captain America goes on countless adventures as leader of the Avengers, but one thing has not changed: Behind Captain America's shield, Steve Rogers is still just a kid from Brooklyn who always does the right thing.

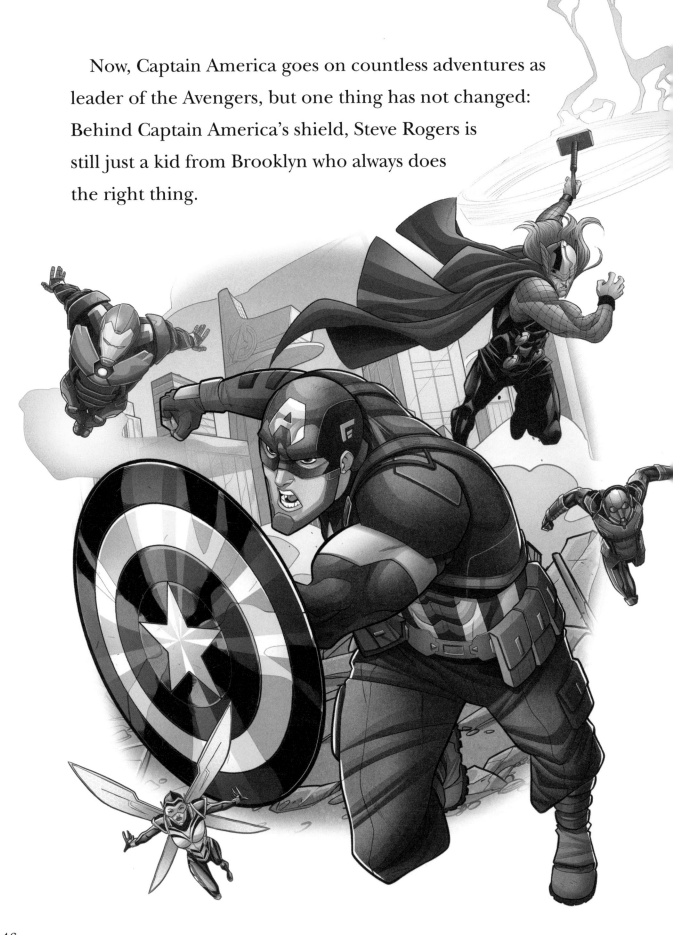

Attack of the Portal Crashers

BOOM! A tremendous noise echoed through the streets of New York City. The ground shook so hard that car alarms went off and stray cats hid under dumpsters.

Spider-Man looked down, his spider-sense on high alert. He immediately spotted Iron Man fighting a strange, feathery villain. It was Spider-Man's old enemy—the Vulture!

Spider-Man swooped in to help.

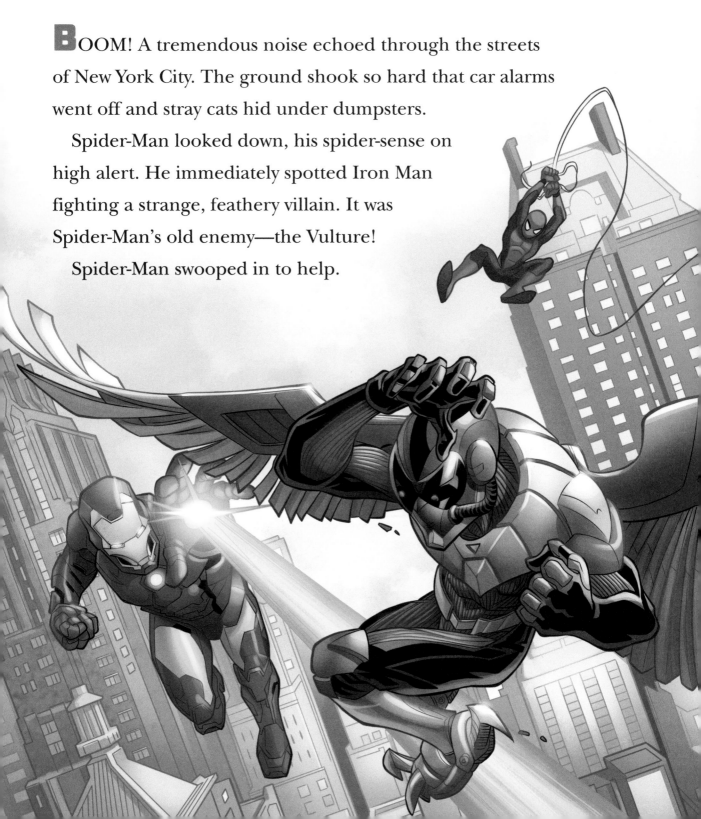

Flying through the city, Iron Man blasted the Vulture, with Spider-Man swinging close behind. The blast hit the villain's legs, and the Vulture fell toward the ground.

At the same time, Spider-Man spun a web to catch the villain.

The city was safe once again. Working together, Spider-Man and Iron Man had beat the Vulture in no time.

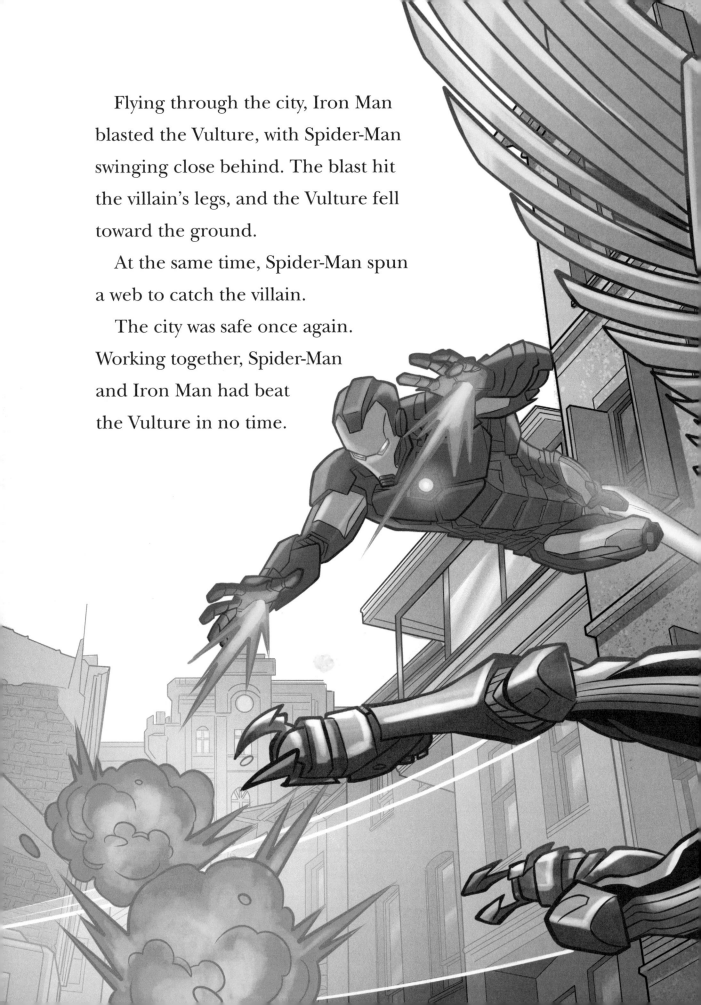

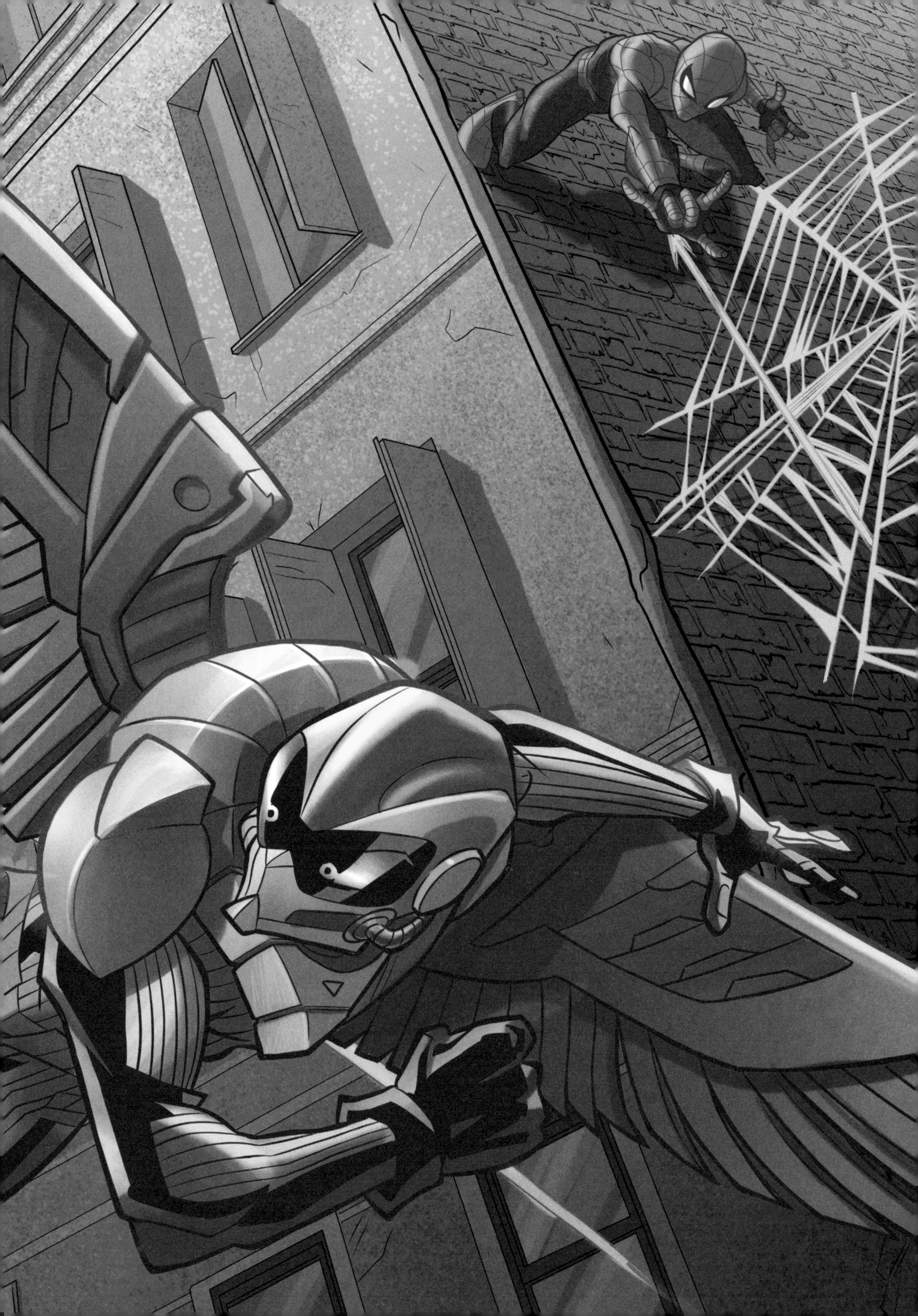

"Thanks, kid," Iron Man said. "We make a pretty great team."

"You're welcome, Mr. Stark," Spider-Man said, blushing under his mask. Iron Man, billionaire Tony Stark, was a big deal.

"Please, Mr. Stark was my father," Iron Man joked. He put his arm around Spidey. "You know, some of the greatest victories have been won by heroes working as a team. Like the time Cap, Falcon, and I teamed up to fight Hydra, or when Widow and Hawkeye took down A.I.M. Cloak and Dagger are always helping Doctor Strange fight Dormammu. Every hero has certain strengths and weaknesses."

"Well, I usually work alone," Spider-Man explained. "I don't think I've earned my place among the real heroes yet."

"There's no shame in needing a little help," Iron Man said with a smile. "See ya around, kid."

As Iron Man rocketed away, Spider-Man began to think about how cool all the other heroes were, and how badly he wanted to prove himself. That gave him an idea. What if he threw a party for them? They deserved it—after all, they saved the world every day.

That night Spider-Man went home and took off his suit. At home he could be just regular old Peter Parker. The more Peter thought about it, the better he liked the idea of throwing a party for the other heroes. *A great party would definitely impress the Avengers!* he thought.

Peter immediately got to work. He wrote invitations to all the Super Heroes he could think of. He knew Central Park would be the perfect place to host the party. He'd bake a cake and maybe even make a piñata. It was going to be awesome!

Peter's invitations made their way to every famous Super Hero in the world.

But one invitation made its way—entirely by accident—through a rogue wormhole right into the hands of Thanos, the cosmic Super Villain.

"All of Earth's Mightiest Heroes in one place?" Thanos said, reading the invitation. "This is my chance to destroy them all in one blow!"

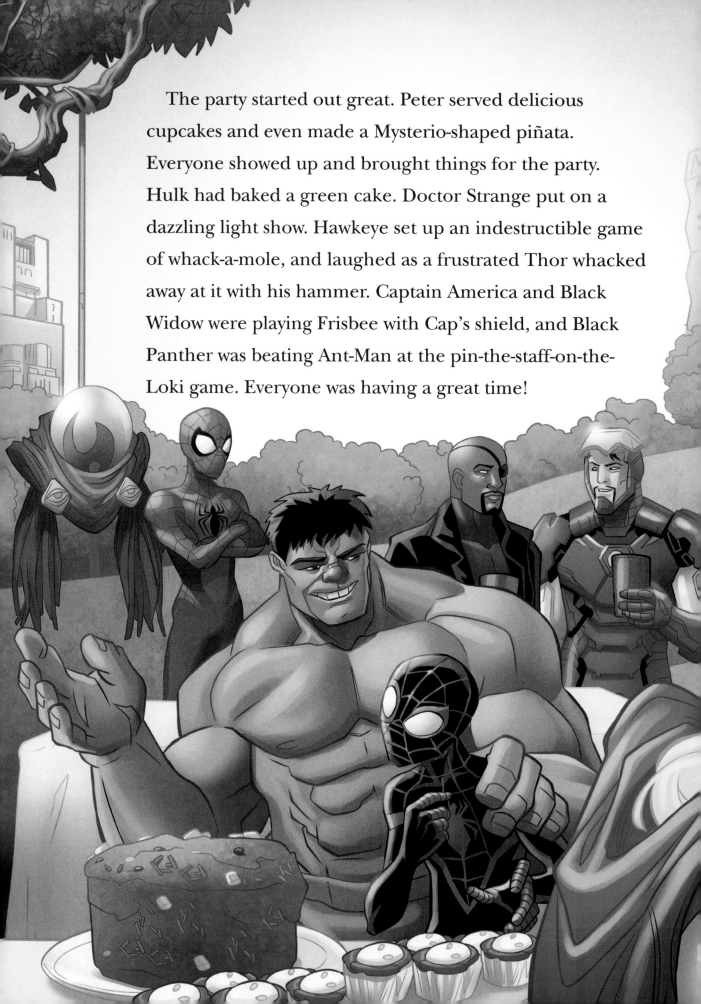

The party started out great. Peter served delicious cupcakes and even made a Mysterio-shaped piñata. Everyone showed up and brought things for the party. Hulk had baked a green cake. Doctor Strange put on a dazzling light show. Hawkeye set up an indestructible game of whack-a-mole, and laughed as a frustrated Thor whacked away at it with his hammer. Captain America and Black Widow were playing Frisbee with Cap's shield, and Black Panther was beating Ant-Man at the pin-the-staff-on-the-Loki game. Everyone was having a great time!

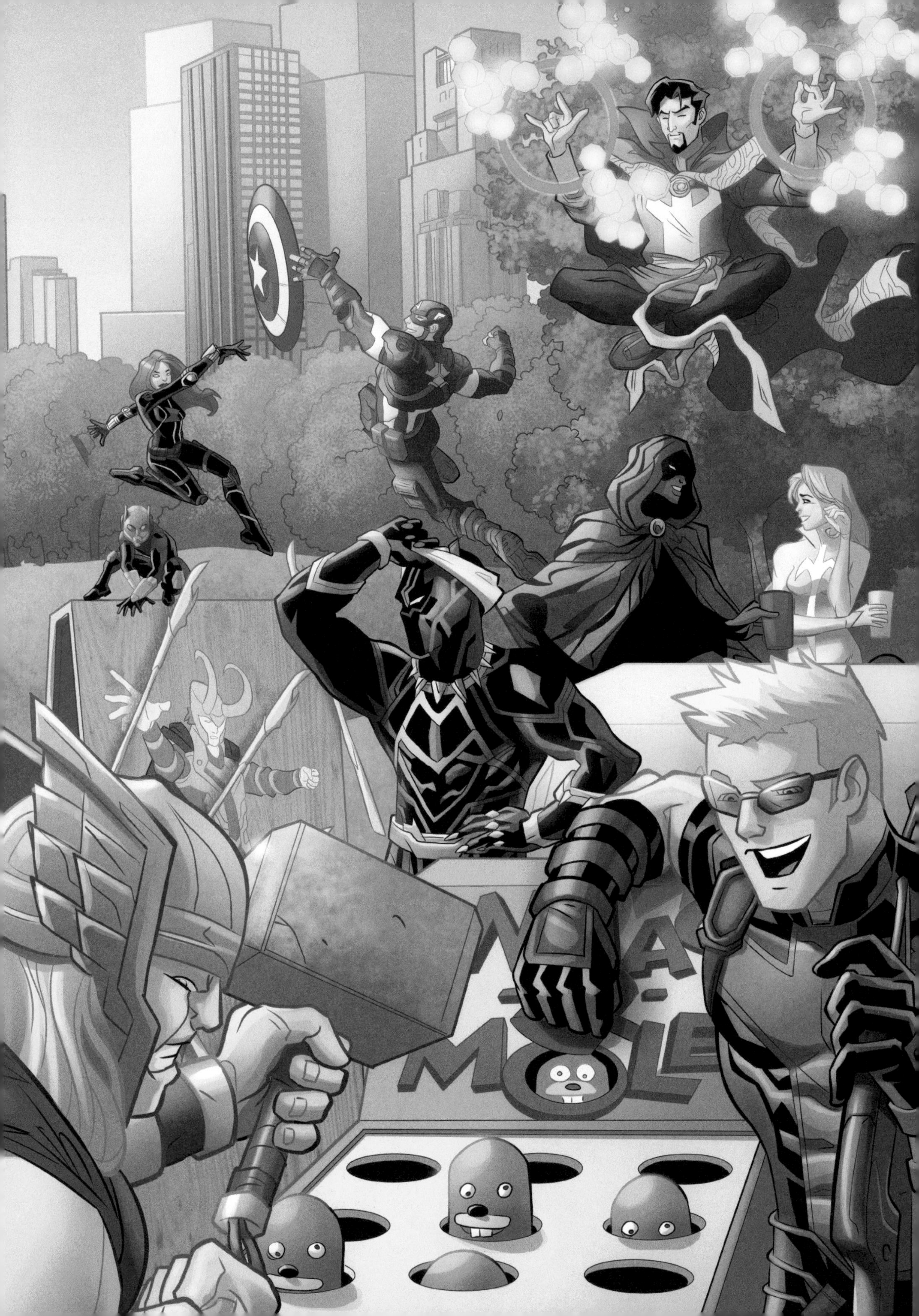

Suddenly the sky turned dark and stormy. Lightning cracked against the gray clouds. "We're under attack!" Captain America shouted as thousands of alien cyborgs started raining down on Central Park.

"It's the Chitauri!" Black Widow yelled.

Every hero leaped into action.

The scene fell into chaos as the world's greatest heroes battled the galaxy's fiercest enemy. With a *zap* of her electrostatic cuffs, Black Widow took out several cyborgs while Thor plowed through another dozen with his hammer. Iron Man and Captain America blasted Chitauri to pieces. Black Panther slashed at them with his Vibranium claws. And as for Hulk . . . well, Hulk SMASHED.

Spider-Man watched in awe. Every hero was needed in this fight—and that included him! He threw himself into the battle, firing webs at lightning speed.

The greatest Super Heroes in the world, including Spider-Man, fought long and hard. Soon the tide of the battle was turning. Fallen cyborgs littered the ground.

But then, with a mighty *CRACK*, the sky split open and Thanos appeared. Spider-Man's heart sank. The Chitauri were bad news, but Thanos was way worse. The world was really in trouble now.

"I've got him!" cried Captain America. But Thanos saw Cap charging and smashed him backward. Then Black Panther leaped at Thanos, kicking powerfully, but the blow bounced right off of Thanos's chest. Doctor Strange's magic couldn't contain the massive villain, and even Hawkeye's sharpest arrow bounced harmlessly away. One by one, the heroes were defeated.

Then Spider-Man remembered what Iron Man had told him:

Some of the greatest victories have been won by heroes working as a team.

That's what they needed! None of them could defeat Thanos alone. But if they teamed up . . .

"Everybody!" Spider-Man cried. "We need to work together!"

With Spider-Man leading the assault, the heroes all fell in. Each hero brought his or her greatest strengths to the fight.

"We need to reverse the portal," Spider-Man realized. "Come on, heroes, let's knock this tough Titan into oblivion!" When the Super Heroes worked as one, they were an invincible army!

In the fiercest battle Central Park had ever seen, Spider-Man and his heroic friends banished Thanos to a far-off dimension in the multiverse. The world was safe.

"Teaching me my own words of wisdom?" Iron Man asked, slinging a metal-clad arm around Spider-Man's shoulders. "You're a pretty smart kid."

"Yeah, maybe even smarter than you." Spider-Man smiled.

"Hey, now, don't get crazy," Iron Man replied.

Spider-Man had finally won his place among the greatest heroes of the age, but it wasn't on his own. Spider-Man teamed up and saved the world!

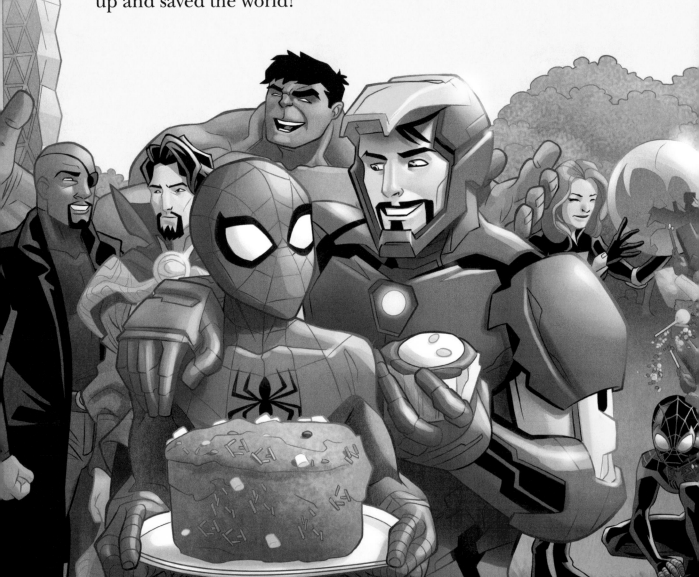

MARVEL
The Switch Up

It was a stormy night as Black Widow and Hawkeye carried out a top-secret mission deep within Hydra's base.

"It's kind of spooky down here," Hawkeye said. "Can we eat after this? I'm starving."

"The sooner we secure the thumb drive with the plans to Hydra's superweapon, the sooner we can eat. It's locked inside this vault," Black Widow replied. "We need to grab it and get out of here."

To unlock the vault, all Hawkeye had to do was say the code words. There was just one problem . . . he'd forgotten what they were.

"Hurry it up, partner," Black Widow said. "We don't have much time."

Hawkeye had been paying attention during the mission brief, but he couldn't remember. "Um . . . open sesame?" he whispered.

"INCORRECT!" the computer snapped.

"If you're not going to take our missions seriously, maybe it's time we took a break from being partners," said Black Widow.

Hawkeye wasn't sure what to say.

"Halt!" a voice called out. Hydra's robot soldiers were on the attack.

Before Hawkeye could reach the exit, a Hydra robot jumped out of nowhere and bonked him on the head.

"Ouch!" he yelped, falling to the ground with a *THUD*. "Wait a minute. Where am I? Who are you? What's going on here?!"

"What?!" Black Widow exclaimed. "Hawkeye . . . please don't tell me you lost your memory."

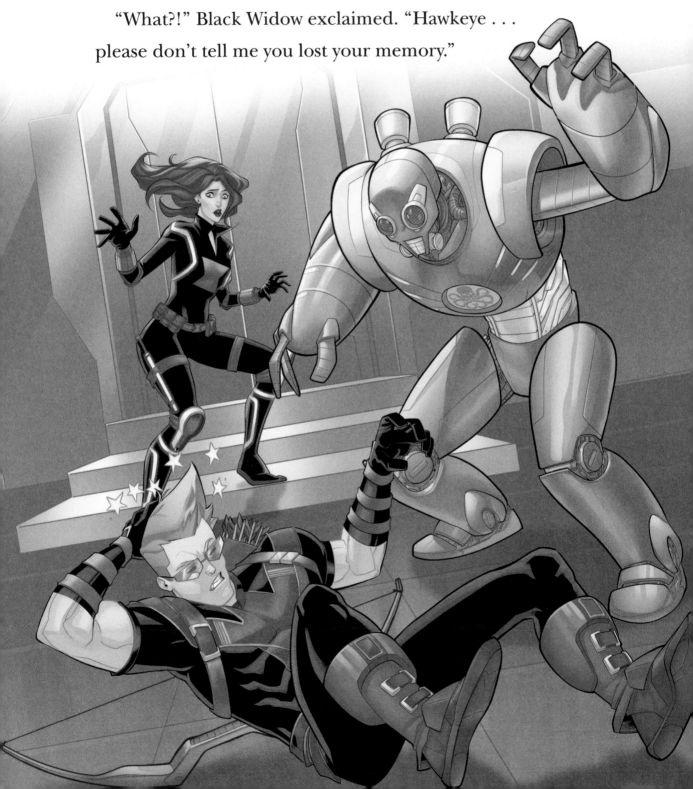

"Who is Hawkeye?" Hawkeye asked, confused.

Before Black Widow could answer, Hydra's robots grabbed the two heroes and tossed them into separate jail cells.

"This is bad," Black Widow said, pacing back and forth. "We need to find a way out of here as quickly as possible."

"I agree . . . uh," Hawkeye said, shaking his head, "what's your name again?"

"I'm Black Widow. You're Hawkeye. We're Avengers," she explained. "You really don't remember anything?"

Hawkeye was confused. "What are we avenging?"

Black Widow reminded her partner about his life as a

Super Hero. She hoped that recounting stories of their adventures together would help jog his memory. "You were the guy who single-handedly stopped Thanos from destroying the planet," she explained. "That's kind of a big deal."

Hawkeye rubbed his chin. "These are great stories. But they're not ringing any bells. Sorry, lady."

Black Widow was at her wit's end. "Don't you remember me? I'm your partner!" she said. "We might argue sometimes, sure, but we've always got each other's backs."

Suddenly Black Widow heard the robot guard's footsteps. It was headed in their direction.

Black Widow climbed up into the ceiling until she was completely out of sight.

"Hey! Where'd she go?" the guard said.

SMACK!

Black Widow swung down from above and kicked the guard in the face. His robot head went flying through the air.

"That takes care of that," said Black Widow.

"Awesome!" Hawkeye cheered. "You're good at this hero stuff."

Black Widow rolled her eyes. "Thanks. I know. Now, follow my lead." She grabbed their weapons, handing Hawkeye his quiver and bow. They ran through the open cell door.

"This tunnel will take us to the roof," Black Widow said. "There's a jump ship up there we can use to escape."

"Wow. You really know what you're doing," said Hawkeye.

Black Widow was all business. "When we get up there, be prepared for anything."

They arrived on the roof to find themselves surrounded by robots once more.

"I'm getting a little tired of this," Black Widow growled.

"What's the plan?" Hawkeye asked.

"The plan is we kick their rear ends," Black Widow said. "Let's dance."

Two Hydra robots sneaked up behind Black Widow and grabbed her on either side. "Find your special arrow with the red tip," Black Widow said, struggling.

Hawkeye spilled his entire quiver full of arrows. "Nuts!" he shouted. He searched through the pile, but he couldn't find the right one.

"We're running out of time," Black Widow said. "I'll just have

Black Widow summoned every ounce of strength she had, smashing the Hydra robots into each other and destroying them in a burst of sparks.

Hawkeye found the red-tipped arrow. "Better late than never, right?"

Another round of Hydra robots was on the move.

"Get it together, Hawkeye!" Black Widow exclaimed. "You're the world's best marksman. It's time you remembered that."

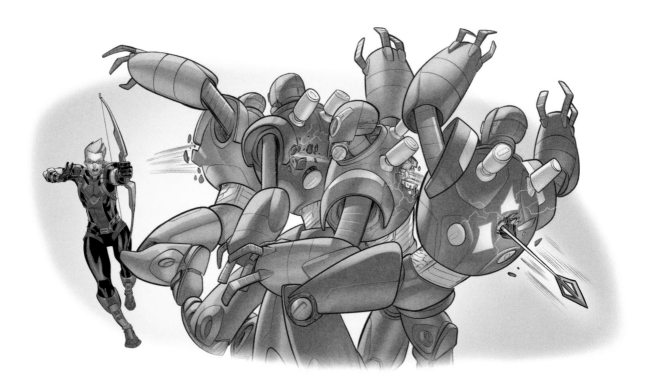

Hawkeye felt a jolt in his brain. His memory had returned at last! His partner's words were exactly what he needed to hear. "Check this out," he said. He shot his arrow through the row of robots like a torpedo.

"Welcome back," Black Widow said. "Took you long enough."

"Tell me about it," Hawkeye said, grinning.

"I just remembered something else!" Hawkeye exclaimed. "Time to get that thumb drive so we can get out of here. Be right back."

"Hurry up," Black Widow said. "We don't have all day."

Hawkeye ran to the vault
and delivered the secret code
words. The door unlocked!
He grabbed the thumb drive,
returned to his partner, and
hopped into the jump ship with
Black Widow "Time to go!"

"You sure you remember
how to fly that thing?" asked
Black Widow.

"Trust me," Hawkeye said.

The heroes settled into the
ship and fired up the engine.
KRACKA-THOOM!

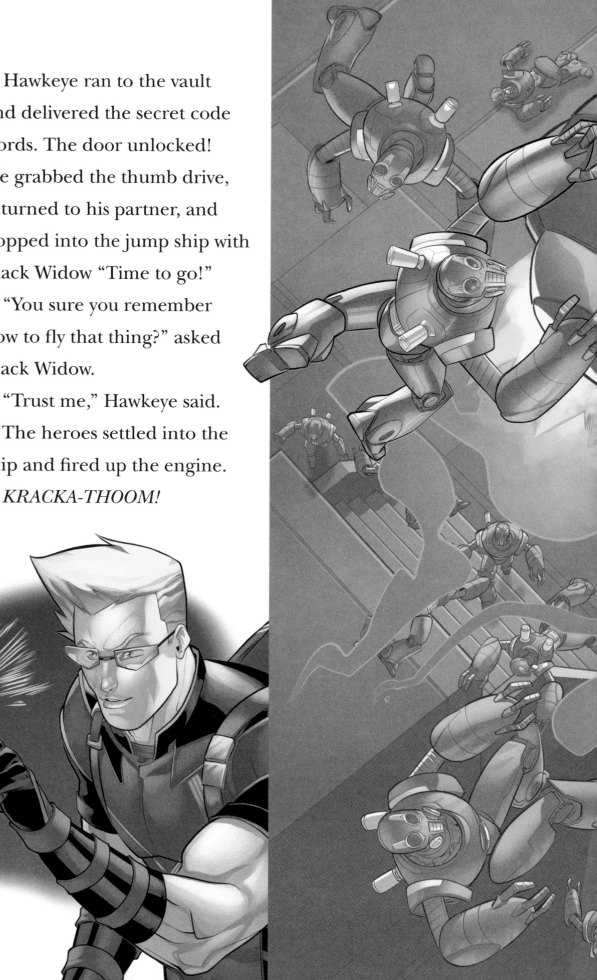

Hawkeye realized he hadn't been the best partner he could have been. "I really messed up, Widow. You had my back, but I didn't have yours," he confessed. "It won't happen again. You have my word."

"Thanks," said Black Widow. "I appreciate that."

GRRRRRR!

A sudden grumbling sound shook the heroes in their seats. "What was that?" Black Widow asked. "Did one of Hydra's robots sneak onto the ship?"

Hawkeye was embarrassed. His stomach was rumbling. "That was me. I'm still hungry," he said, chuckling. "Can we stop at the nearest taco truck? That is, if you don't mind."

"You got it," Black Widow replied. "Anything for my partner."

Full Force!

Carol Danvers was having a blast as her jet soared through the clouds above a classified air field. An ace fighter pilot for the U.S. Air Force, she was the best of the best—and that was no secret.

Carol worked hard protecting her country from every type of threat. She worked hard to save lives and protect her fellow soldiers, and the United States was safe thanks to Carol Danvers.

Eventually, NASA heard about Carol Danvers and her stellar military record. The agency recruited her to be the Head of Security, protecting the United States from cosmic threats. In her new position, Carol learned not only that aliens were real but that many of them were bent on destroying Earth!

One of those alien races was the Kree Empire. NASA was
concerned that their endless galactic wars were making Earth
vulnerable to alien attacks. So Carol invited the Kree leaders to
NASA Headquarters. She knew she needed to form an alliance
with the Kree. The safety of the planet was at stake.

During the meetings, Carol was pleasantly surprised to find she was becoming fast friends with the Kree dignitaries, especially their central leader, Captain Mar-Vell. However, that would not last long. One of the Kree, the evil Yon-Rogg, did not want peace. So he came up with a plan.

Under the cover of darkness, Yon-Rogg captured Carol along with a powerful alien device he had taken from the Kree ship. It didn't take long for Captain Mar-Vell to find them and launch an epic attack! During the battle, the alien device erupted, creating a massive explosion that engulfed everyone. Even Carol Danvers.

In the aftermath, Carol escaped unhurt and Yon-Rogg was never seen again. Captain Mar-Vell and his fellow Kree left Earth to continue their galactic wars. Although the peace mission was a failure, Carol knew that working with the Kree had been the right thing to do.

Weeks later, Carol began to feel strange. One night, she felt dizzy until the world suddenly went black.

The next thing Carol knew, she was floating!
She felt powerful and could create sparkly
energy with her hands. Carol Danvers had
transformed into a super human. And eventually
she would become known as Captain Marvel!

The explosion had awakened Carol's super-powers! She started to test her powers and found she could fly through the air just by thinking it! By tightening her fists, she could send blasts of powerful photon energy. She could even absorb different types of energy and use it to enhance her already-powerful superhuman abilities. Captain Marvel had become stronger, faster, and virtually indestructible!

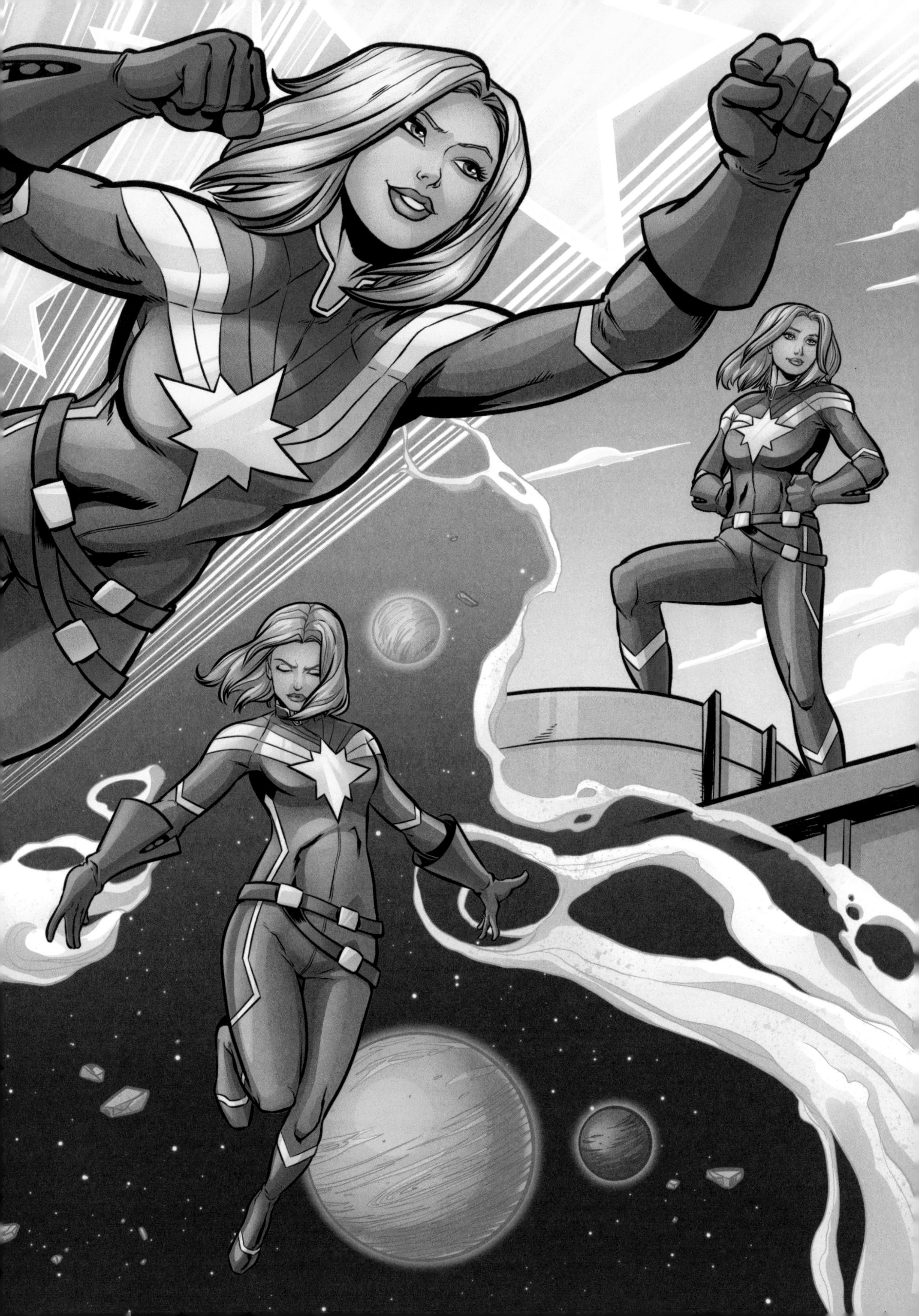

As a Super Hero, Captain Marvel was able to do things she'd only dreamed of as a pilot. She took to the skies, exploring the far reaches of space and using her powers for good. Along the way, she met new friends . . . and new enemies. But in the end, something always pulled her back home.

There was no mistaking it: Captain Marvel's military training had made her Earth's fiercest protector. Whether it was a meteor hurtling through Earth's atmosphere or a galactic council meeting, Captain Marvel always wanted to protect her home.

After saving the world many times, Captain Marvel was recruited to lead the Alpha Flight Space program. Alpha Flight was created as Earth's first line of defense against alien threats. As lieutenant commander, she was able to prevent a massive attack from an evil alien army, the Chitauri.

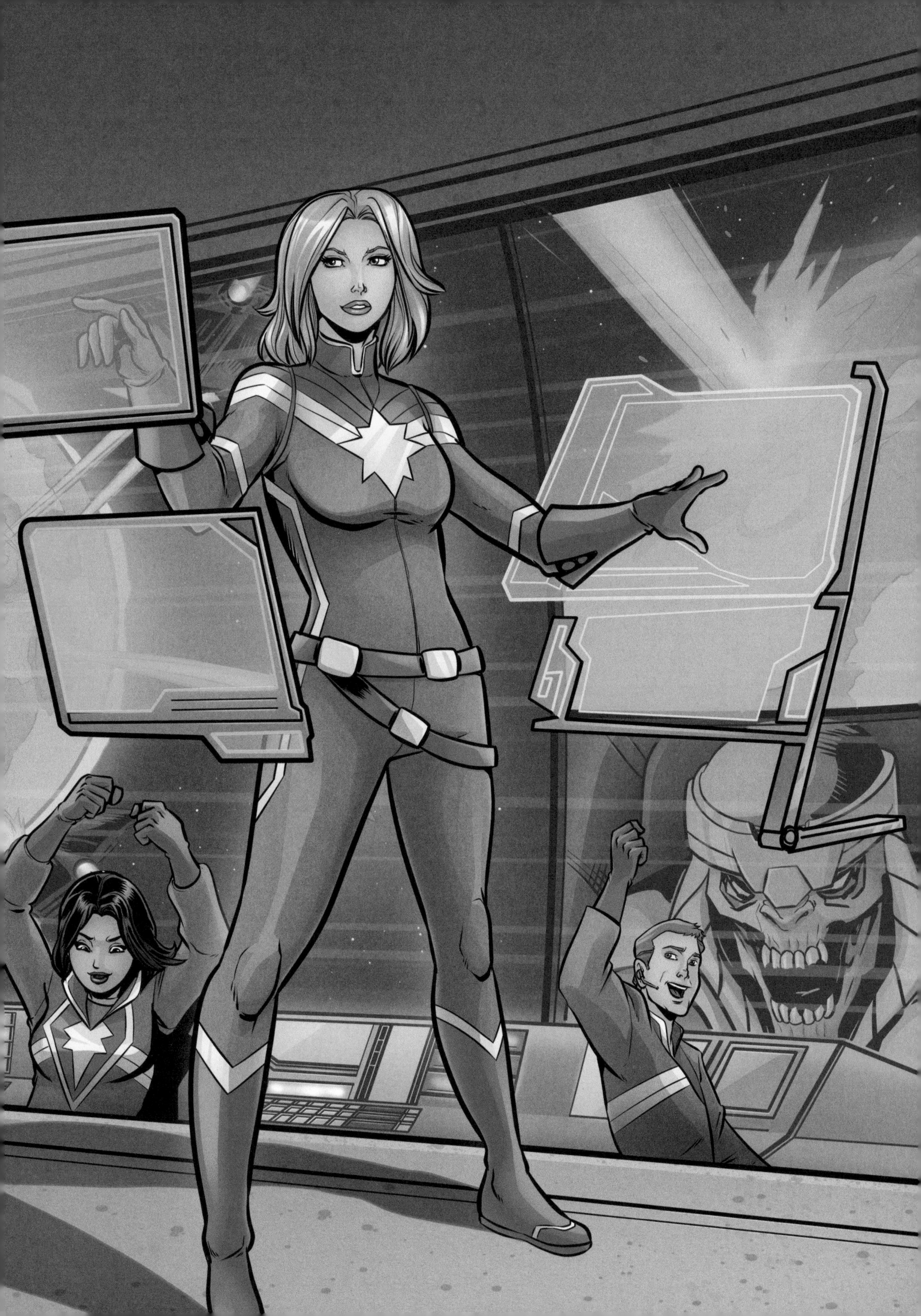

In addition to working for Alpha Flight, Captain Marvel also teamed up with other Super Heroes to defend the world. One of those teams was Earth's Mightiest Heroes—the Avengers! Their missions took Captain Marvel all over the world and into the cosmos. But when the job was done, Captain Marvel always returned home to Earth and her Alpha Flight crew. Whether flying solo or with her fellow heroes, Captain Marvel was a force to be reckoned with!

Rocket Science

"This place stinks!" Rocket shouted. After a very long journey, the Guardians of the Galaxy had finally arrived on a strange planet called Blorf. They were there to pick up a package for one of their clients. The heroes looked out on the eerie landscape from their spaceship, the *Milano*

Star-Lord was excited for a new adventure, but Gamora was already anxious to leave. "Let's get what we came for and be gone," she said. Drax nodded his head in agreement.

Rocket sniffed the air around him. "Not only is this planet a dump but so is our spaceship," he said grumpily. "It needs a good scrub."

"Good thinking, Rocket," Star-Lord said. "Why don't you stay behind and clean it up?"

A big grin appeared on Groot's face. He loved Star-Lord's idea. "I am Groot!"

While Groot was excited, Rocket didn't like Star-Lord's idea one bit. "But I wanted to come with you guys!" he yelped.

"No *buts*," said Star-Lord. "Somebody needs to do it. You should stay inside while we're gone. You never know what creatures might be lurking around."

Drax smirked as Rocket continued to whine. "We'll be back soon, tiny rodent."

Rocket hated being left behind to do the team's dirty work. "Star-Lord has got a lot of nerve telling *me* what to do!" Rocket grumbled. "Did everyone bang their heads and forget I'm a genius?!"

Groot put his hand on Rocket's shoulder, hoping to calm him down. "I am Groot," he said softly.

Suddenly Rocket had a bright idea.

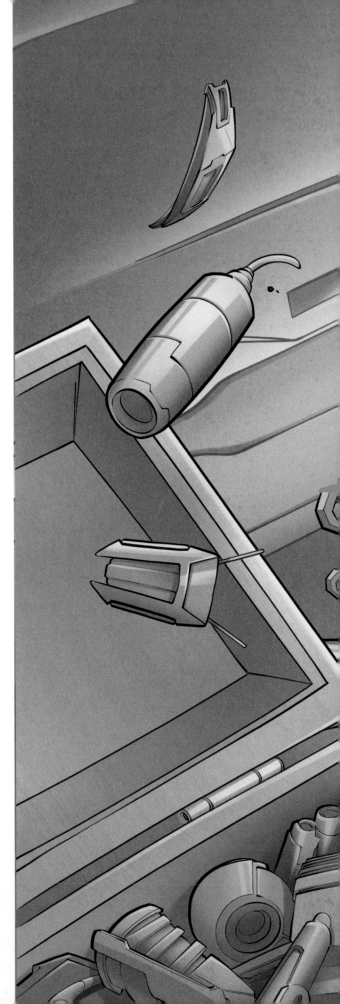

"Groot, old buddy, you and I are going to find a way to make this place sparkle without having to lift a finger," Rocket said. "How does that sound?"

Groot wasn't sure what to say. He just shrugged.

"There's an old cleaning bot we can use to do all the work," Rocket said, impressed by his own quick thinking. "It's in my box of special science stuff." He hauled out a giant crate filled with hundreds of gadgets and began to rummage.

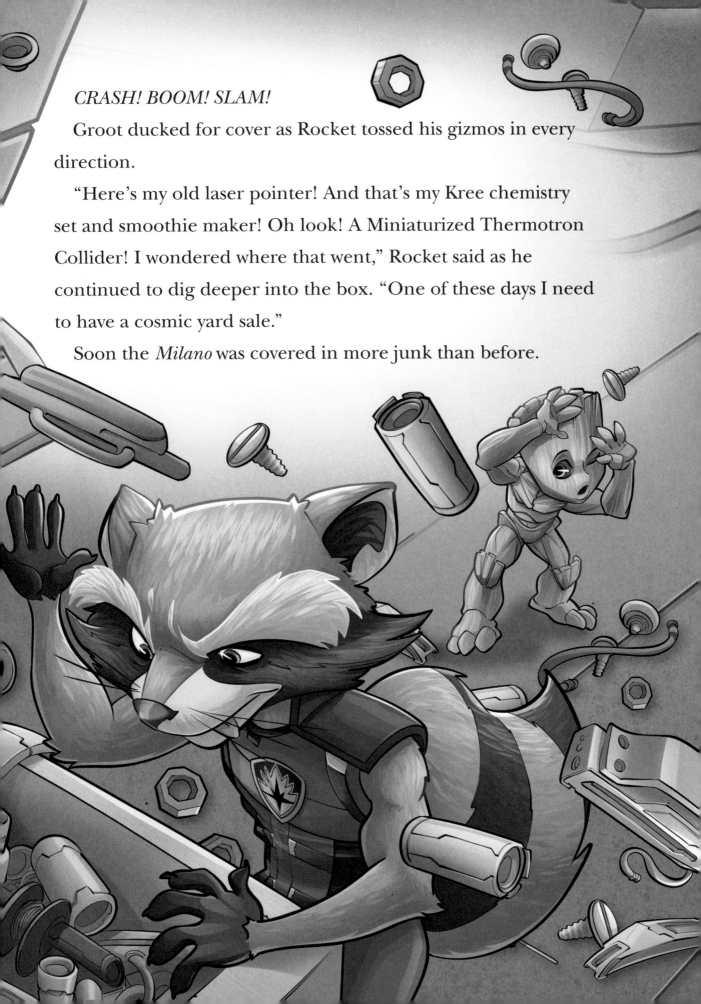

CRASH! BOOM! SLAM!

Groot ducked for cover as Rocket tossed his gizmos in every direction.

"Here's my old laser pointer! And that's my Kree chemistry set and smoothie maker! Oh look! A Miniaturized Thermotron Collider! I wondered where that went," Rocket said as he continued to dig deeper into the box. "One of these days I need to have a cosmic yard sale."

Soon the *Milano* was covered in more junk than before.

"Here we go! Come to Papa!" Rocket exclaimed, reaching into the box. He held a clunky contraption in the air like a trophy. "It's my old size-changing ray! Let's see if I can get this thing working." He pressed a few buttons.

SHAZACK!

Suddenly a purple laser blasted from the size-changing ray and hit Groot right in the belly, causing him to grow bigger.

"I am Groot?" he asked.

"Ugh. The settings must be off. Let me try again," Rocket said. The size-changing ray fired once more.

SHAZACK!

This time it made Groot enormous.

"I am Groot!" he exclaimed.

Rocket was flustered. He desperately tried to fix the broken device. "This should do the trick," Rocket said. The size-changing ray fired once more.

SHAZACK!

With that, Groot returned to normal size.

Rocket set aside the size-changing ray. "Come on, let's find that cleaning bot and get this show on the road."

As Rocket looked through the box of science stuff, Groot opened up a storage locker to find the cleaning bot staring back at him. "I am Groot!" he exclaimed.

"Well, what do you know?" Rocket said.

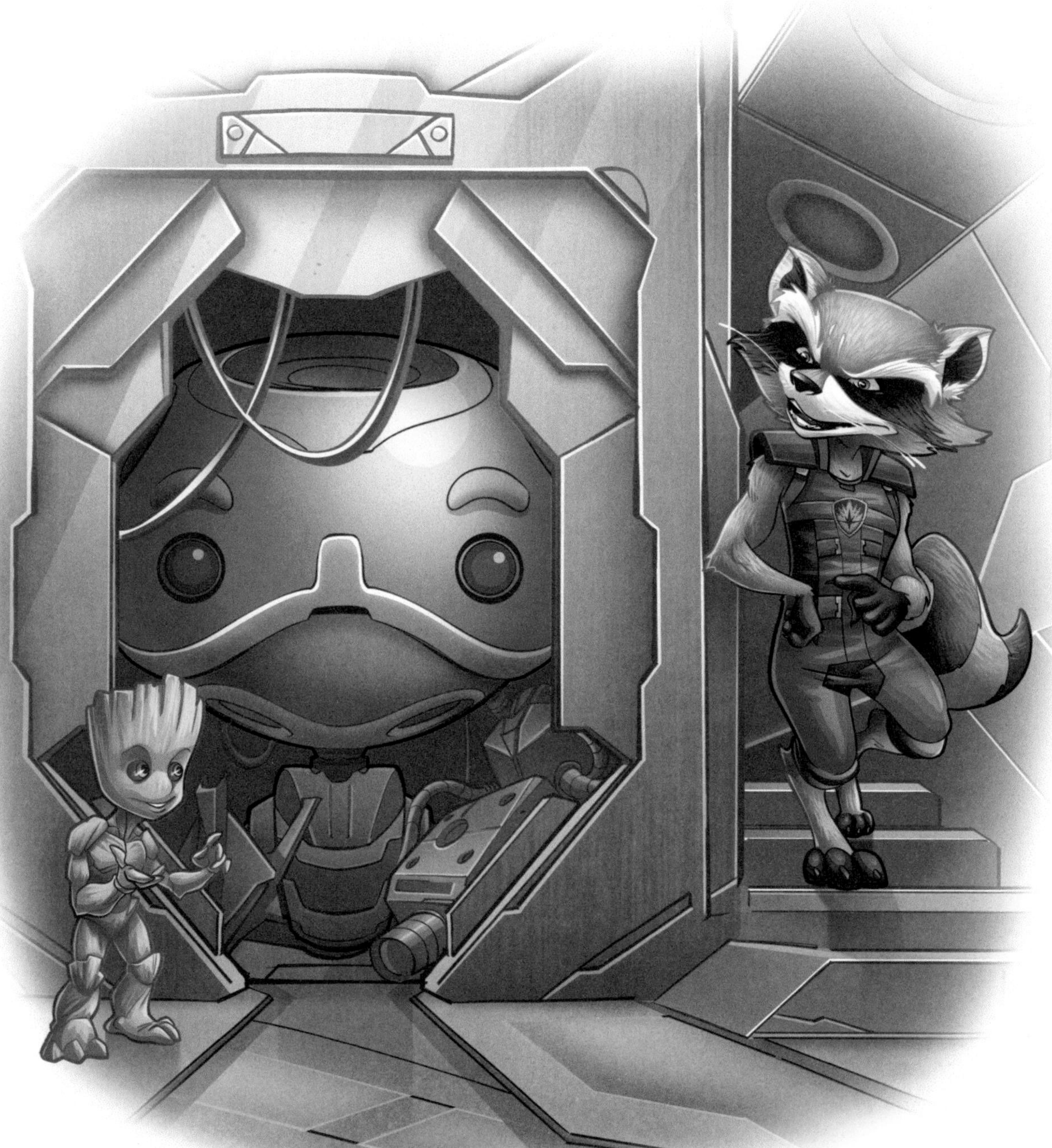

"Let's do this!" Rocket exclaimed. He turned
a knob on the back of the bot, and a jumble of
mechanical arms appeared out of nowhere. "Uh-oh."

The bot started screeching, "MALFUNCTION!
MALFUNCTION!"

Instead of cleaning the *Milano*, the bot began smashing
everything to bits. Almost all of Rocket's science stuff had
quickly been turned into scrap metal.

Before Rocket could corral the crazy robot, it opened the *Milano*'s door all by itself and went outside! "Oh no you don't," Rocket said.

"I am Groot!" Groot exclaimed.

On the surface of Blorf, the cleaning bot's commotion attracted a group of funny-looking pig-like aliens called the Kodabaks. Snorting in excitement, the Kodabaks picked up a giant net, thinking they could take the bot home as a pet.

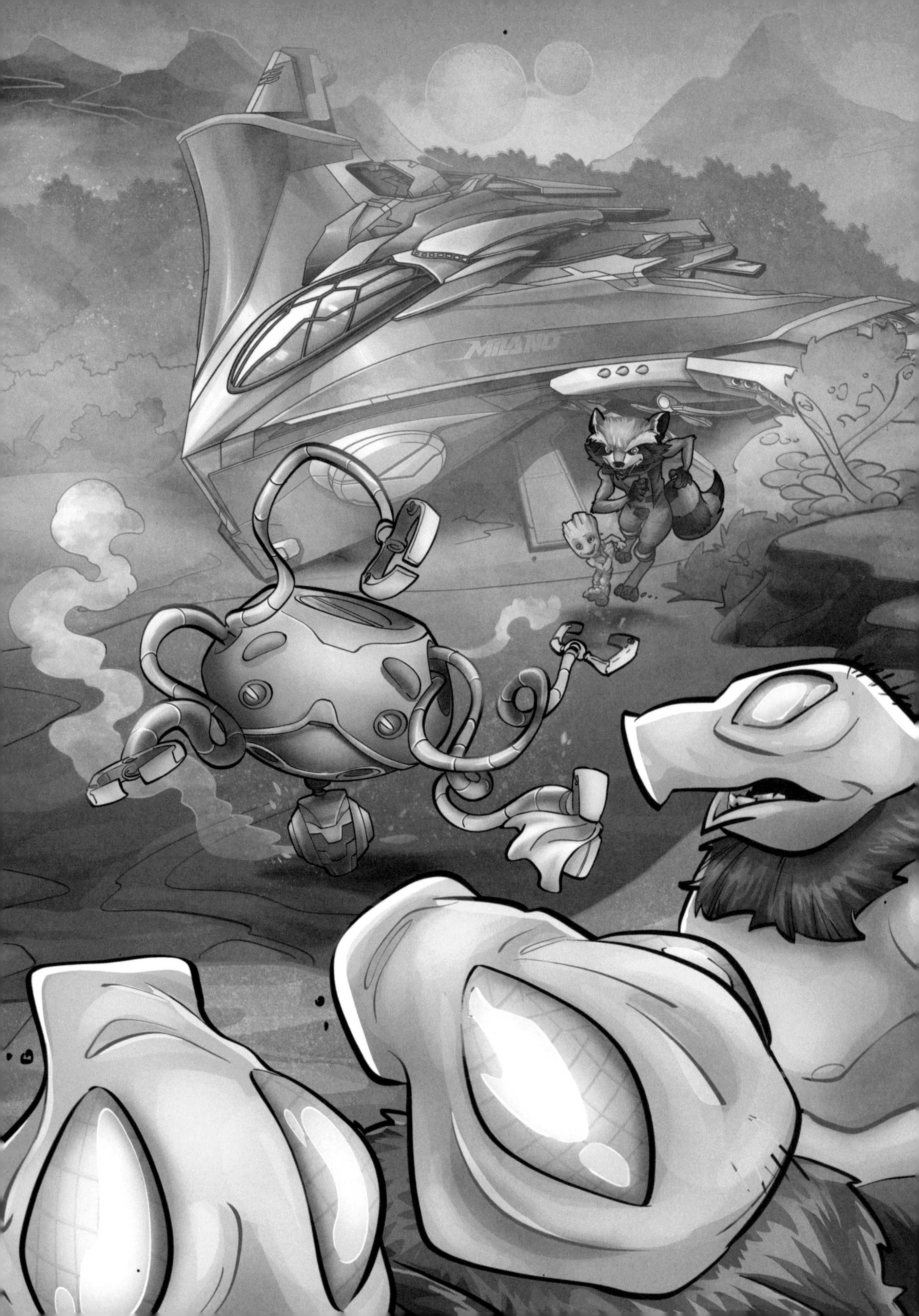
MILANO

Rocket wasn't sure what to do. But luckily
Groot had a suggestion. "I am Groot!" he exclaimed.

"That's a great idea! Thanks, buddy!" said Rocket. He
grabbed his size-changing ray and aimed it at the Kodabaks.
"You feeling lucky, pigs? I know I am."

SHAZACK!

Rocket blasted the beasts with purple energy, shrinking them
down. "Take that!" he said with a smirk.

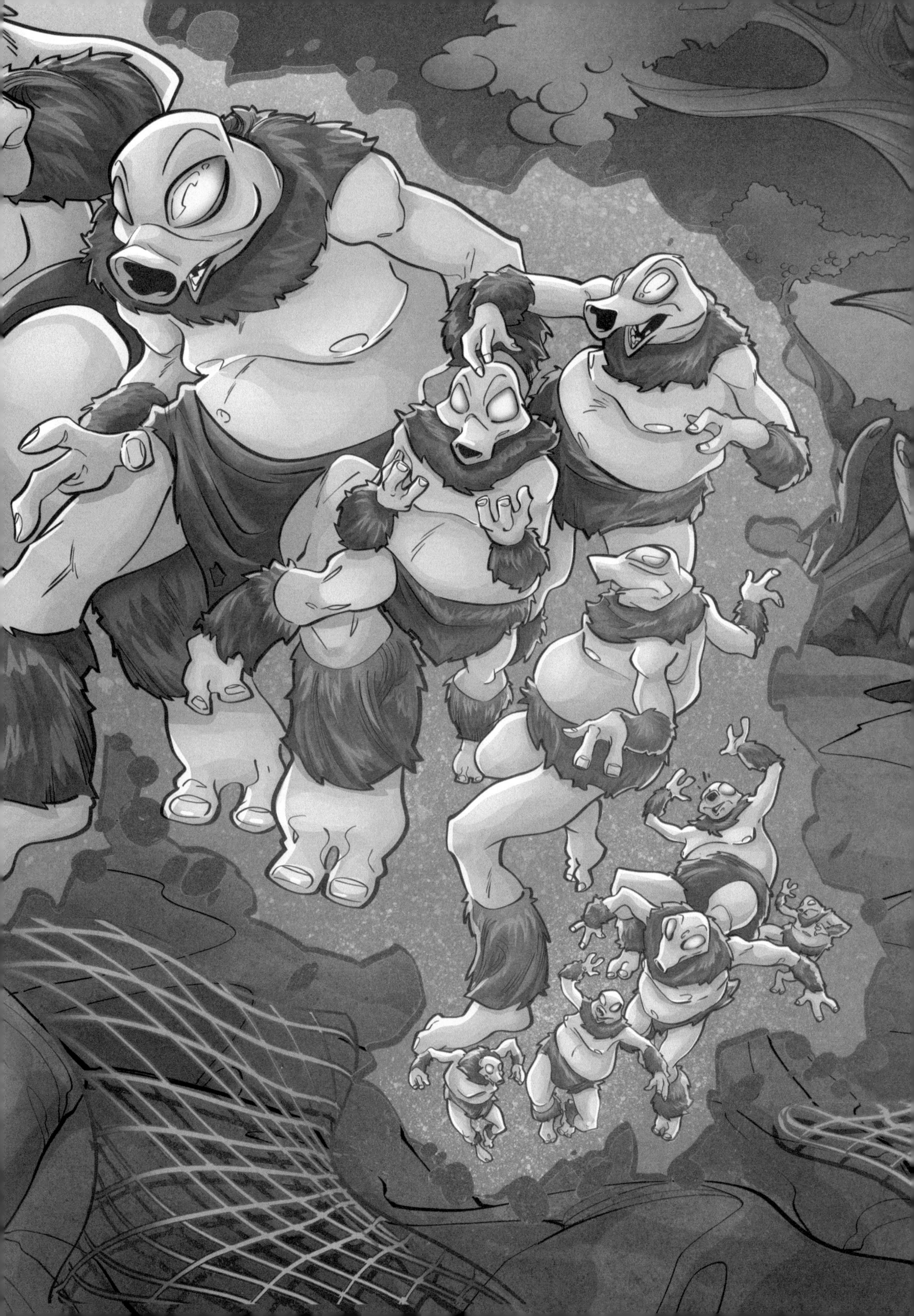

"This is my chance to save the day! I've got to act fast," Rocket said. With tool in hand, he jumped onto the bot's back. In an instant, it was fixed. "Watch this!"

The cleaning bot swept the tiny Kodabaks up into its dustbin without a second thought. Then the bot raced into the *Milano* as quick as lightning.

"Look at it go!" Rocket shouted.

In a matter of minutes, the cleaning bot washed the entire ship from top to bottom. It even took out the trash and recycled the metal waste. At last Rocket could breathe. "Would you look at that!" he shouted. "Clean as a whistle."

"I am Groot," said Groot.

When Star-Lord, Gamora, and Drax returned from their mission, they were impressed by how clean everything looked.

"Nice work, Rocket," Star-Lord said. "The *Milano* looks great."

Rocket grinned. "I can't take all the credit," he said, picking up Groot. "After all, I *did* have a little help."

Island of the Cyborgs

Captain America was on a solo mission. A ship carrying high-tech battle gear had disappeared, and Nick Fury had tasked him with finding it.

Cap entered the ship's last known coordinates into his Quinjet and took off. Soon, he found himself flying over an island with what appeared to be an abandoned fortress on it. He landed with a splash in the water and began to make his way to land.

Captain America had been on enough missions to know that just because something *looked* abandoned didn't mean it actually was. He approached the fortress slowly and quietly.

Suddenly—*PEW! PEW! PEW!* The beach lit up with hundreds of bright green blasts. Cap was under attack!

The powerful blasts were no match for Captain America's Vibranium shield, but they were still strong enough to throw him to the ground. Finally, they stopped. Cap struggled to get up, straining to see through the dust and debris.

Then, in the distance, he spotted a strange shape.

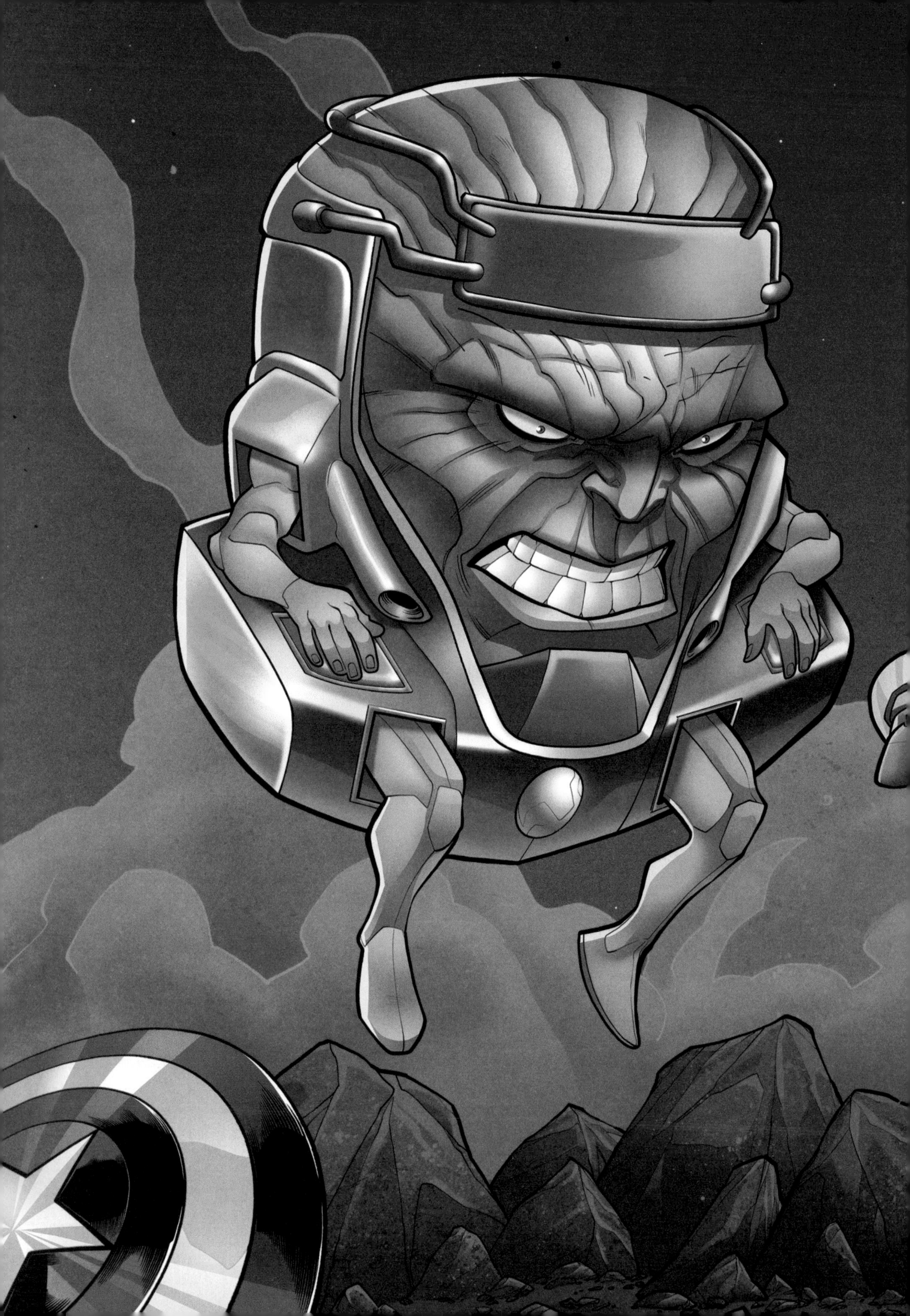

As the shape moved closer, Captain America realized it was M.O.D.O.K., a genetically engineered, superintelligent being bent on destroying the world. But the Super Villain wasn't alone. He was surrounded by an army of creatures wearing the missing battle gear.

Cap did a double take as he looked more closely at what was piloting the suits. "Monkeys!" he shouted. "Now, that's a first!"

The monkeys seized Captain America and threw him into a prison cell.

"You came to save the day, and instead you get a front-row seat to watch as I take over the world!" M.O.D.O.K. taunted.

"World domination," Cap said. "Very original. But why monkeys?"

"Primates are easy to control," M.O.D.O.K. replied. "And even easier to find in large numbers . . ."

Cap looked out his window. To his dismay, he saw thousands of armed monkeys, ready to do M.O.D.O.K.'s bidding.

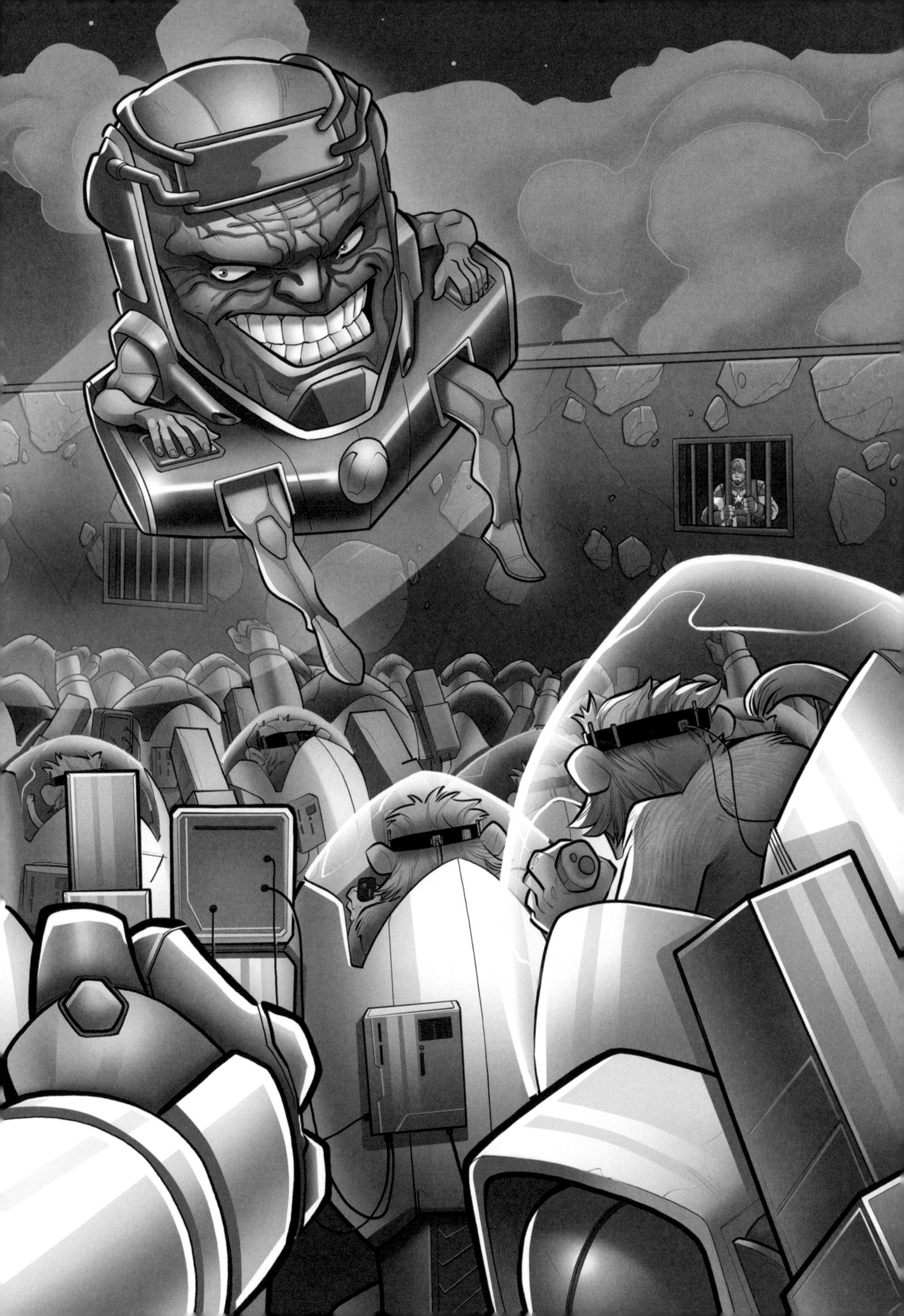

Captain America sat back down in his cell, disheartened. But he couldn't give up. He needed to fight back! That gave him an idea. "Hey, ugly!" Cap shouted at one of the cyborg monkeys walking by his cell. "I call this one Monkey See, Monkey Do!"

The hero began to slam his metal cuffs against the metal bars of the cell. The sound vibrated through the stone walls. The cyborg monkey started to twitch and reared its head—the loud noise was driving him crazy. He began to claw at the metal bars. Anything to make the sound stop.

His battle suit bent the bars enough that he pulled himself inside the cell with Captain America. With a screech, the cyborg monkey lunged at the hero!

Cap moved out of the way as the cyborg grabbed his chains, twisting and breaking them into pieces. Captain America's plan

Thinking quickly, Cap vaulted through the cell opening and bent
the bars of the cell, trapping the cyborg. He turned toward the
massive lab. "Now if I were a Vibranium shield, where would I be?"

Captain America quickly found his shield, but he froze as a
giant hand landed on his shoulder. It wasn't a human hand—it
was much bigger, heavier, and stronger.

Cap now found himself face-to-face with an army of cyborg monkeys. He punched one cyborg and was surprised when its battle suit exploded. A frightened monkey scurried out of the broken machine.

Cap realized that M.O.D.O.K.'s mind control only worked on the monkeys when they were inside the suits! He quickly set about destroying every single cyborg in the lab. Pieces of their battle suits littered the floor as the monkeys escaped the fortress unharmed.

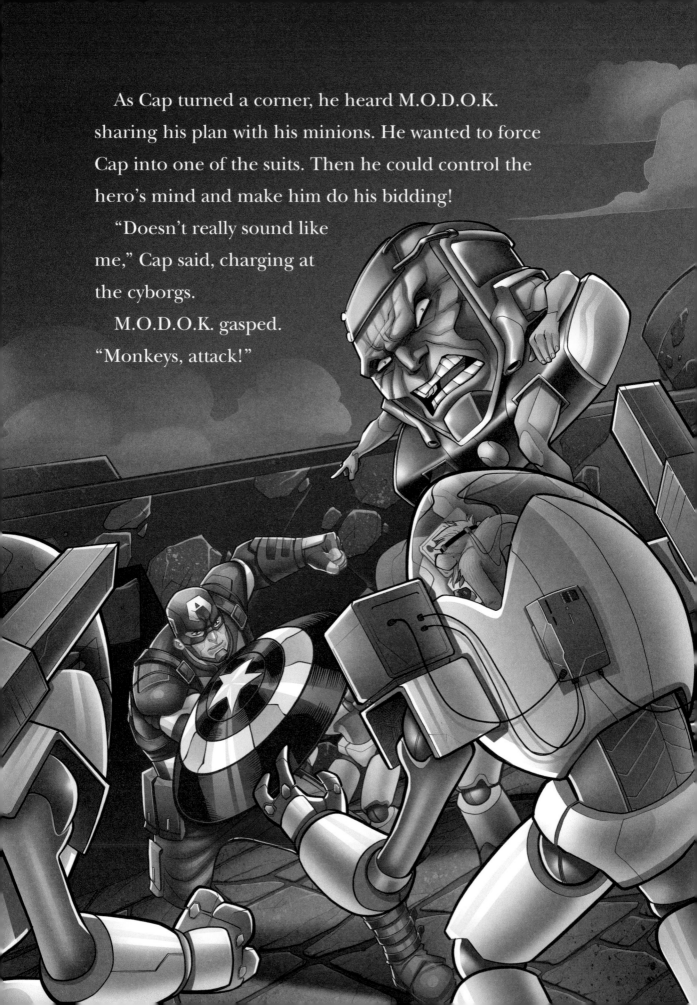

As Cap turned a corner, he heard M.O.D.O.K. sharing his plan with his minions. He wanted to force Cap into one of the suits. Then he could control the hero's mind and make him do his bidding!

"Doesn't really sound like me," Cap said, charging at the cyborgs.

M.O.D.O.K. gasped. "Monkeys, attack!"

Captain America knew he couldn't stop thousands of cyborgs on his own. But he could stop M.O.D.O.K. Cap knew from previous battles that if he broke the Super Villain's chair, he would break the mind-control connection.

The hero pushed his way through the cyborg monkeys until he found an opening. Taking aim, he threw his Vibranium shield at M.O.D.O.K. The villain crashed into the ocean below. Cap looked over the wall for any sign of M.O.D.O.K., but he was gone.

Captain America set about releasing the remaining monkeys.
He was just breaking the last few suits when a message came in.

"How'd we do?" Nick Fury asked.

Captain America smiled. "M.O.D.O.K. is gone. For now, anyway."

"Great," Nick replied. "I have another solo mission for you and
I need you at attention, soldier. No more monkeying around!"

Iron Man: Invincible!

As a boy, Tony Stark dreamed that technology could change the world for the better. Tony was just nineteen years old when he started designing cutting-edge machinery for his family's company Stark Enterprises. "This has got to work," Tony declared as he built new gadgets.

But to create them, Tony would need money, space, and resources. The United States Army was happy to give him everything he needed as long as Tony would give their soldiers better weapons.

The army commanders asked Tony, already the head of Stark Enterprises, to teach their soldiers how to use his weapons to keep evil forces at bay. "All you need to do is put your hands like so, point it toward the bad guys, and grin ear to ear, because you're about to make the world a safer place," Tony told the soldiers to raucous applause.

As much as the troops loved Tony for making their jobs safer,
the warlords on the other side of the mountains hated him.
Without warning, an attack broke out! The soldiers defended
Tony well, but one of Tony's own devices exploded—he was
blasted off of his feet and felt a sharp pain in his chest before
he slammed into the ground. "AAAARGH!" The last thing Tony
remembered was a loud ringing in his ears.

When Tony woke up, he was surprised to see a smiling face looking down at him. "My name is Dr. Ho Yinsen," the smile said. "You're safe for now, but the explosion lodged shrapnel close to your heart." Yinsen had created a powerful magnet that would pull on the shrapnel, preventing it from killing Tony.

Tony was confused. "I— Thank you, Yinsen," he said. Tony wasn't used to thanking other people. But before the two men could continue getting to know each other, several warlords barged into the cave where Tony and Yinsen were trapped.

"Stark and Ho," one of the warlords bellowed. "Two of the world's smartest men. You will build weapons for us. And maybe we will let you live in return. Ha ha ha!"

After the warlords left the room, Tony turned to Yinsen. "What do you say," Tony asked as he smirked. "Should we give them new weapons?"

"Yes," Yinsen said, "I think we should. But I don't think they're going to like it." They set to work right away, gathering supplies from the tools and equipment the warlords had brought them.

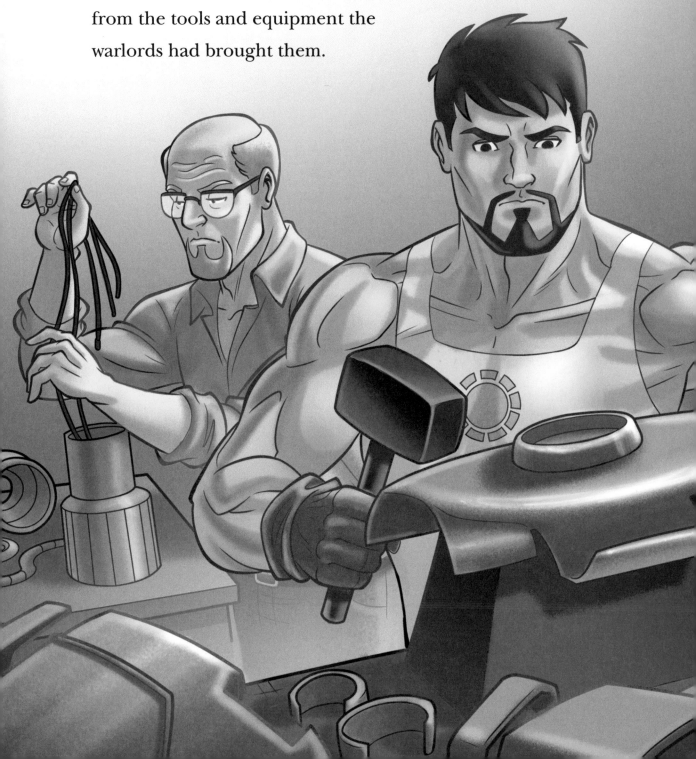

It took weeks, but both men worked very hard, eager to be set free. Large pieces of gray metal were coming together, and they had a power source to run the behemoth. When their time was up, they sprung their plan!

As the warlords approached, Tony strapped himself into his weapon. It wasn't some kind of ray gun or rocket; it was a powered-up battle suit. Yinsen took cover as Tony smashed through their prison door and declared, "I AM IRON MAN!"

The warlords' weapons hardly made a dent in the gray armor! Iron Man was invincible! "Hey, guys," Tony joked, "I've got a few ideas for upgrades on your weapons systems. Too bad for you, I used them on this armor instead!" He charged toward the warlords and they turned, fleeing in fear.

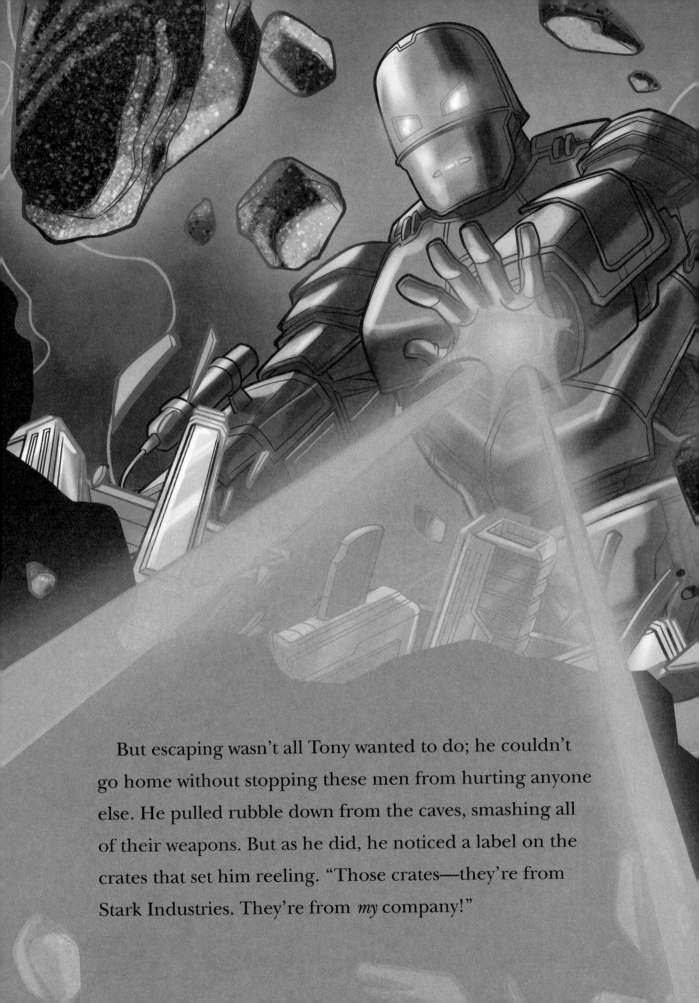

But escaping wasn't all Tony wanted to do; he couldn't go home without stopping these men from hurting anyone else. He pulled rubble down from the caves, smashing all of their weapons. But as he did, he noticed a label on the crates that set him reeling. "Those crates—they're from Stark Industries. They're from *my* company!"

Tony felt ashamed that his work was being used by warlords. But along with his shame, Tony also felt something new. There was just a spark of it—a hint of pride that, at least in this one instance, he had taken weapons away from bad men.

Tony made it out of the cave, but Yinsen didn't make it out. "You saved my life, Dr. Yinsen. I can't be a part of hurting more people—I see now that my work creating weapons has hurt a lot of people."

Upon returning home, Tony made a public promise. He said, "Stark Industries will never sell weapons to anyone again. And not only that, I'm putting all of my engineers and scientists—and myself—to work creating things that will make the world better, smarter, and safer!"

Tony believed that just stopping the creation of new weapons wasn't enough. So he kept working in secret to refine and re-design his Iron Man armor so he could protect the world from the weapons he wouldn't be able to stop.

Tony continuously upgraded his armor over the next several years. He fought tirelessly to keep the world safe. Eventually, he became a founding member of the Mighty Avengers!

Tony Stark wouldn't be remembered for his time creating weapons. Instead, the world came to know him for his red and gold armor. The world soon called him a Super Hero—the Golden Avenger. He was Tony Stark—the Iron Man!

MARVEL

The Hunt for Black Panther

Kraven the Hunter loved to hunt wild animals. The only thing he loved more than hunting was the fame that came along with it. But one day, after Kraven had captured a pair of cheetahs, he didn't feel the same sense of accomplishment he normally felt after a successful hunt.

Kraven hungered for a new prey that would give him a real challenge. But where could he find such a foe?

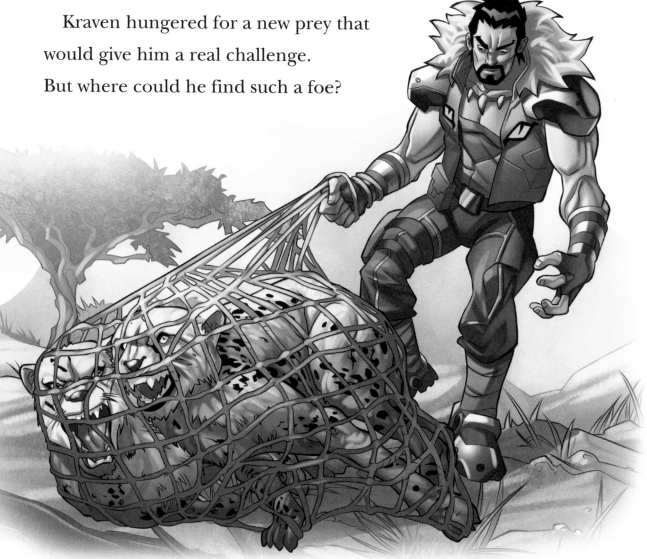

A few days later, Peter Parker was sent by the *Daily Bugle* to photograph the annual Protection of Endangered Animals conference in Upper Manhattan. Giving the keynote speech was none other than T'Challa, ruler of the African nation of Wakanda.

Peter was excited about the opportunity to actually see T'Challa speak. The king was a compassionate ruler and a scientific genius.

But T'Challa had a secret. He was also the Super Hero Black Panther!

"In order to protect the animals of Earth," the king began, "it is our duty to fight back against illegal hunters and poachers."

Black Panther protected his nation and its animal kingdom from villains by using his superhuman strength, speed, and agility. One of those villains was Kraven the Hunter.

Craving a new challenge, Kraven knew that this conference was the perfect place to find his next prey—Black Panther! The villain burst through the window in a spray of broken glass.

"T'Challa!" he bellowed. "I request a meeting with the Black Panther."

T'Challa's eyes narrowed. "Black Panther will never bow to the likes of you!"

Kraven smirked. "I assumed there would be some protest."

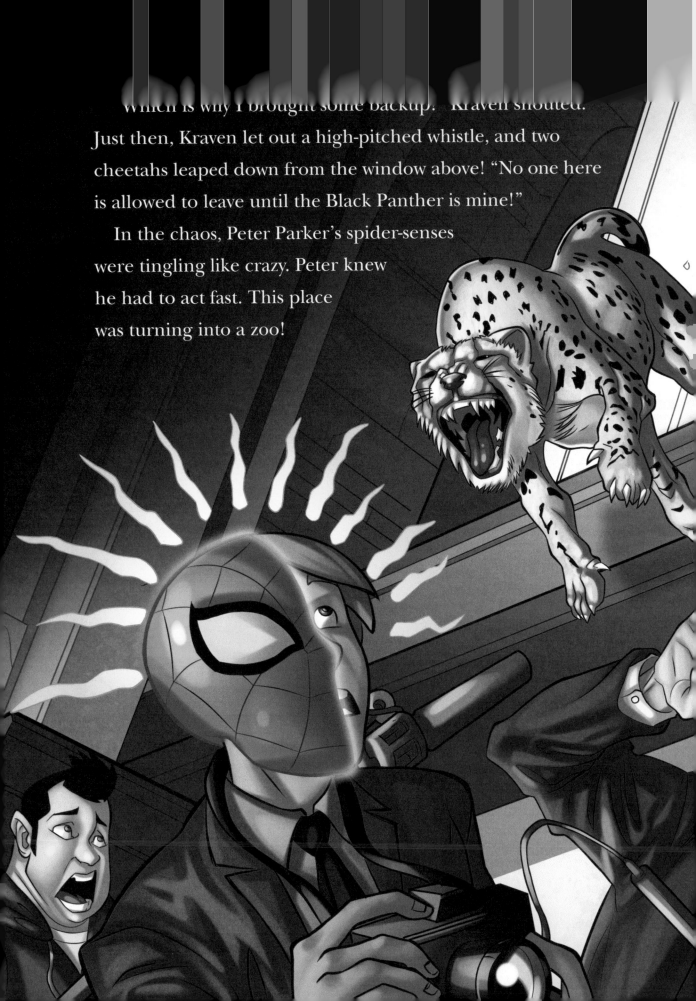

"Which is why I brought some backup!" Kraven shouted. Just then, Kraven let out a high-pitched whistle, and two cheetahs leaped down from the window above! "No one here is allowed to leave until the Black Panther is mine!"

In the chaos, Peter Parker's spider-senses were tingling like crazy. Peter knew he had to act fast. This place was turning into a zoo!

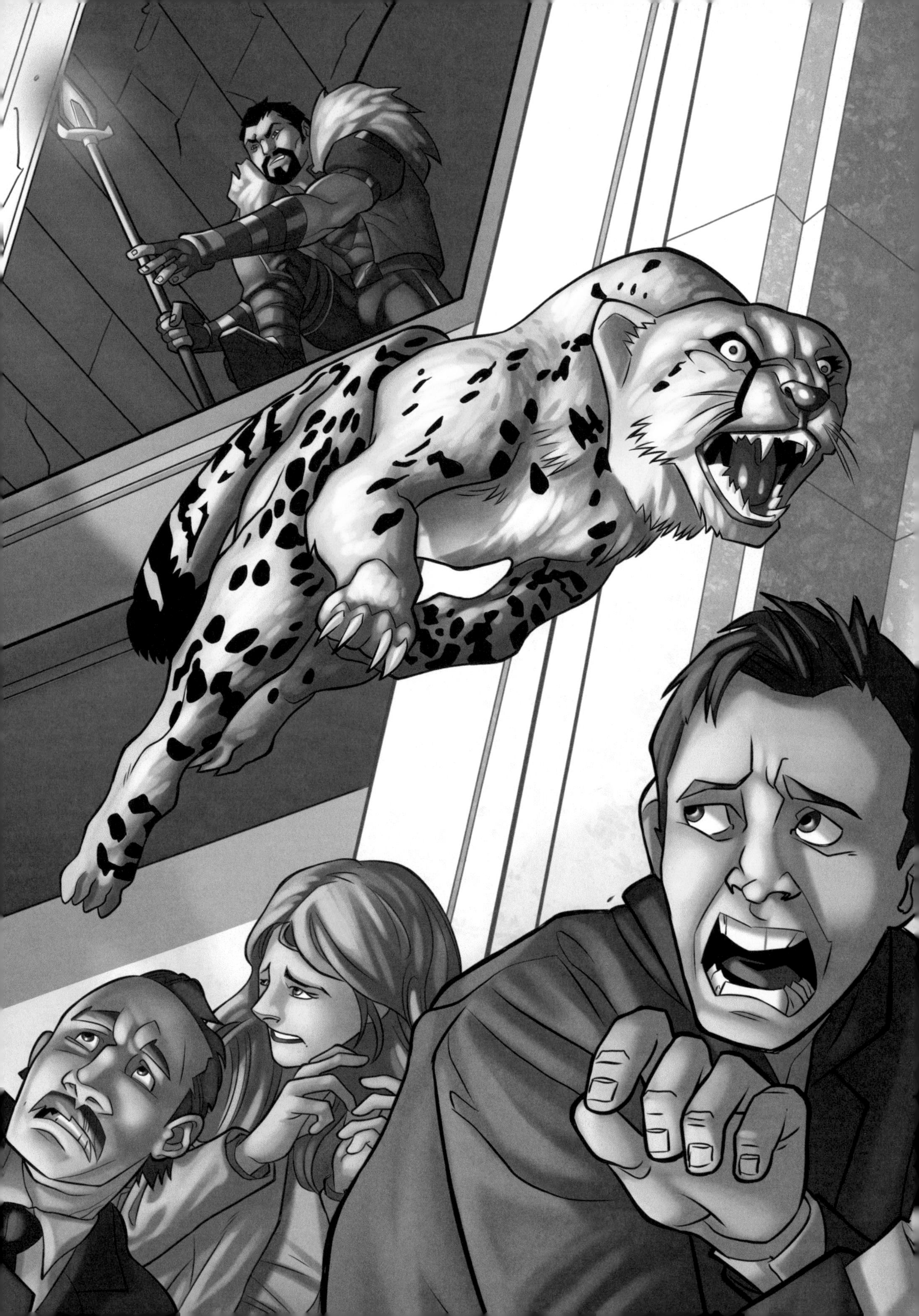

Meanwhile, T'Challa's bodyguards, the Dora Milaje, attempted to move the Wakandan king to safety.

"Save your energy," he commanded. "It's time for Black Panther to strike."

Black Panther turned around to discover he had been joined by Spider-Man!

"What are you doing here?" Black Panther asked.

"Nice to see you, too," Spider-Man said as he fired a ball of web fluid at the nearest cheetah. "Stand back—I've beaten Kraven before. I can deal with these overgrown house cats."

"Spider-Man, no! You must be careful!" Black Panther tried to warn the web-slinger, but it was already too late.

"Whoa! Nice kitty!" Spider-Man exclaimed as the cheetah grabbed his web and lunged toward him.

Acting fast, Black Panther grabbed the cheetah before Spider-Man was harmed. "Listen to me. My animal instincts tell me that these creatures are being held here against their will. They will only attack you if they are provoked."

But Spidey wasn't out of danger yet! Kraven threw a spear at the web-slinger, but Spidey rolled out of the way just in time!

"I'll calm them down while you get Kraven," Black Panther said to Spidey.

"On it!" Spider-Man said as he swung toward the balcony.

While holding back the cheetahs, Black Panther massaged the backs of their heads. Kraven had found a way to increase the aggression of these animals. Luckily, Black Panther was more familiar with wildlife. He safely pressed down on the cheetahs' pressure points to relax the animals' anger.

"That should calm you down," he said, petting the cheetahs.

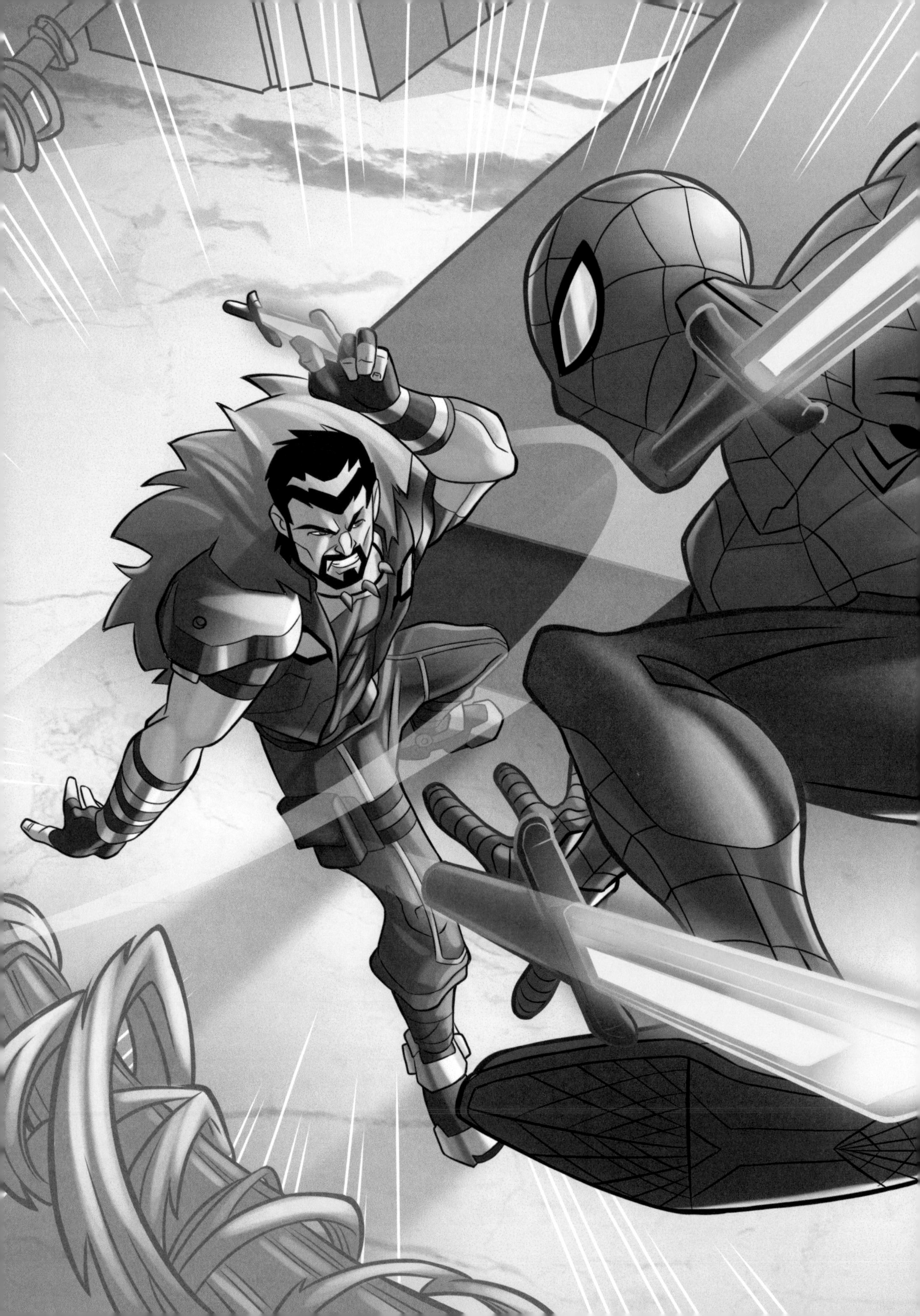

With the cheetahs under control, Spider-Man caught up with the villainous hunter.

"You are nothing but a minor nuisance. I did not come here for you, but if I must capture you, too, so be it!" Kraven said. He began throwing knives at the web-slinging hero. Unfortunately for Kraven, Spidey's trusty spider-sense made it impossible for him to land an attack.

"What's the matter, Kraven?" Spider-Man asked. "Can't catch a little spider?"

"Maybe it would help if you took care of that smell first, Kraven. P-U! Or do they not have showers in the jungle?" Spider-Man joked.

Blinded with anger, Kraven was unable to focus on the fight with the two Super Heroes. Spider-Man quickly used his web-shooters to disarm Kraven, giving Black Panther the perfect opening for an attack.

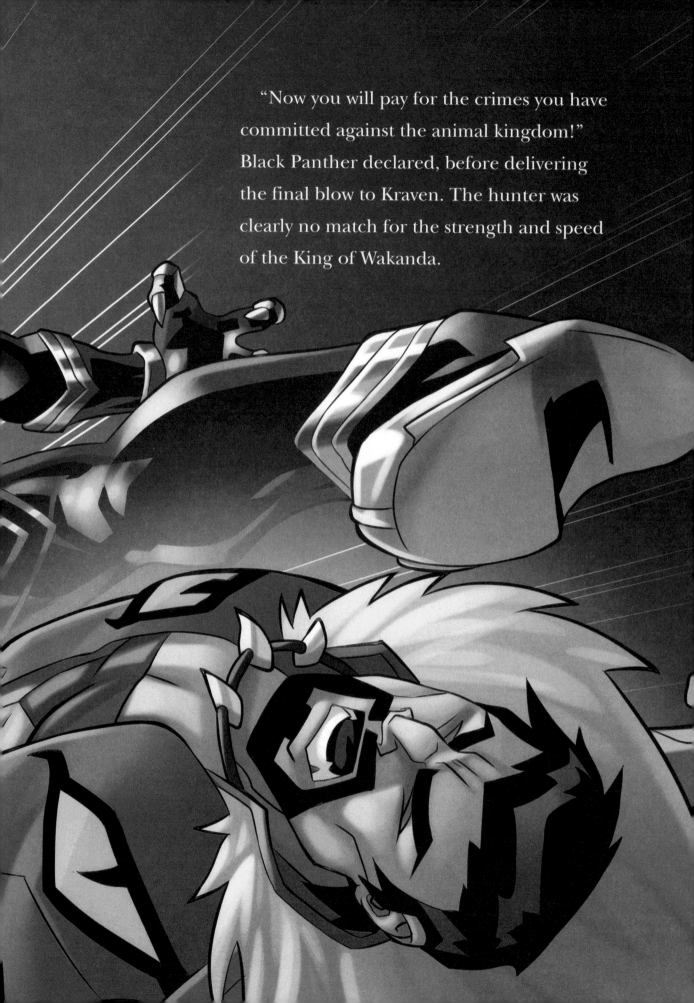

"Now you will pay for the crimes you have committed against the animal kingdom!" Black Panther declared, before delivering the final blow to Kraven. The hunter was clearly no match for the strength and speed of the King of Wakanda.

Kraven was finally defeated.

"Beaten by a spider and a cat," he mumbled.

"What's wrong? Don't like being held in captivity?" Spider-Man asked.

Black Panther addressed the crowd of frightened spectators. "You are all safe! These majestic creatures are not the enemy. They deserve respect and compassion. And thank you, Spider-Man, for helping me save them."

Spider-Man was caught off guard by the Black Panther's kind words. "Wow. Thanks, Black Panther. Now might not be a good time, but do you mind if we take a selfie?"

Mixed Signals from Knowhere

On Knowhere, Drax was lost in his thoughts. He turned into one of the depots and didn't even notice the supply clerk smiling at him.

"What's got you down?" the clerk asked. Drax jumped, surprised. The supply clerk looked ridiculous. She was almost lost among a clutter of recycled machinery, wires, and space gadgets. She seemed to be wearing some of it, too.

"I . . . I am not down," Drax replied. "You are the one who is down. You are very short."

"Ha, you're funny!" she said. "I'm Kaz, by the way."

"Kaz," Drax repeated. "That is a silly name. I am Drax."

She laughed again, and this time, Drax smiled.

"Drax—that's a cool name," Kaz said. "Are you from Knowhere?"

Drax suddenly remembered he had somewhere to be. "I should be going."

Kaz nodded, and Drax saw the look of disappointment in her eyes. Without thinking, he continued, "Do you want to come with me?"

Kaz smiled. "Sure!"

Drax led her back to the *Milano*, enjoying the way she laughed at everything he said.

The other Guardians were surprised when Drax introduced his new friend.

"I am Groot," Groot said, extending his branch to Kaz.

Rocket smirked. "Maybe she can help me with one of my gadgets."

"Nice to meet you," Gamora said simply.

Star-Lord was not as friendly. "Not suspicious at all," he muttered to himself. "It's not like we have mystery people trying to sneak onto our ship here. . . ."

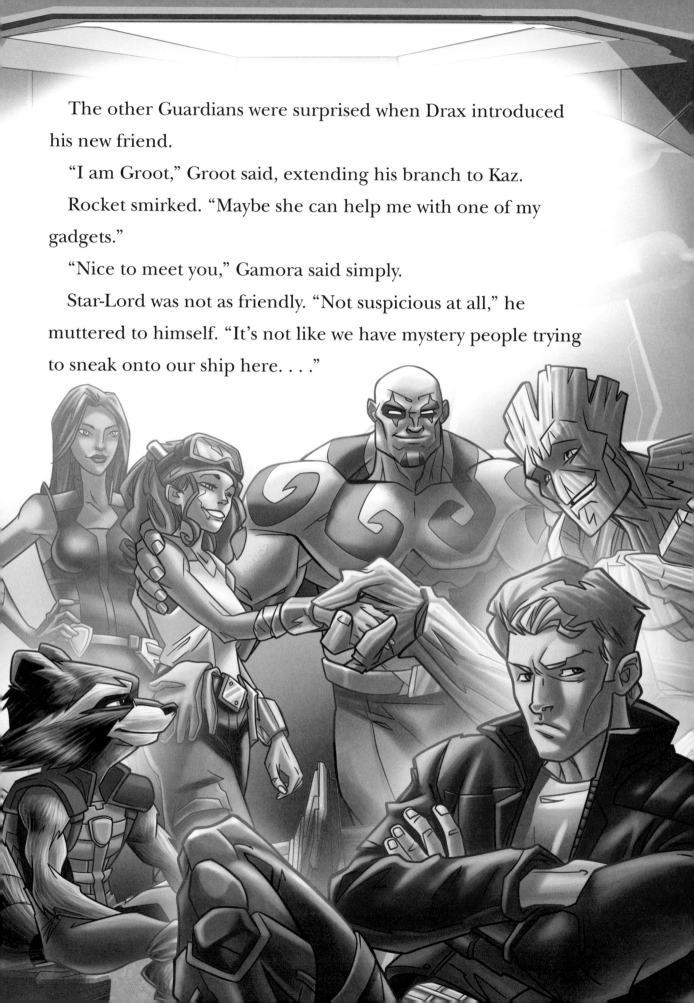

Just then, the emergency
distress signal started to beep.

Star-Lord rushed over to the communication
console, where Rocket was already intercepting the message.

"It's coming from right here on Knowhere," Rocket relayed.

"Well, is it somewhere or nowhere?" Drax asked.

"It's somewhere on Knowhere," Gamora interjected.

The look on Kaz's face turned to alarm. Star-Lord narrowed
his eyes at her. "You wouldn't happen to know anything about
this, would you?" he said.

Just then, a huge blast shook the *Milano*! It knocked the Guardians and Kaz off their feet. Outside, burning embers and smoke still billowed from the blast. Star-Lord led the Guardians to go investigate.

Star-Lord looked up to see Iron Man, one of Earth's mighty
Avengers.

"Oh, good," Star-Lord said. "Reinforcements!"

"I don't think he's here to help," Gamora said, as Iron Man
turned and fired a huge blast at a building. "He's attacking!"

"I am Groot!" Groot said.

"I know, pal. He may be a good guy," Rocket replied, "but right
now he's on a rampage."

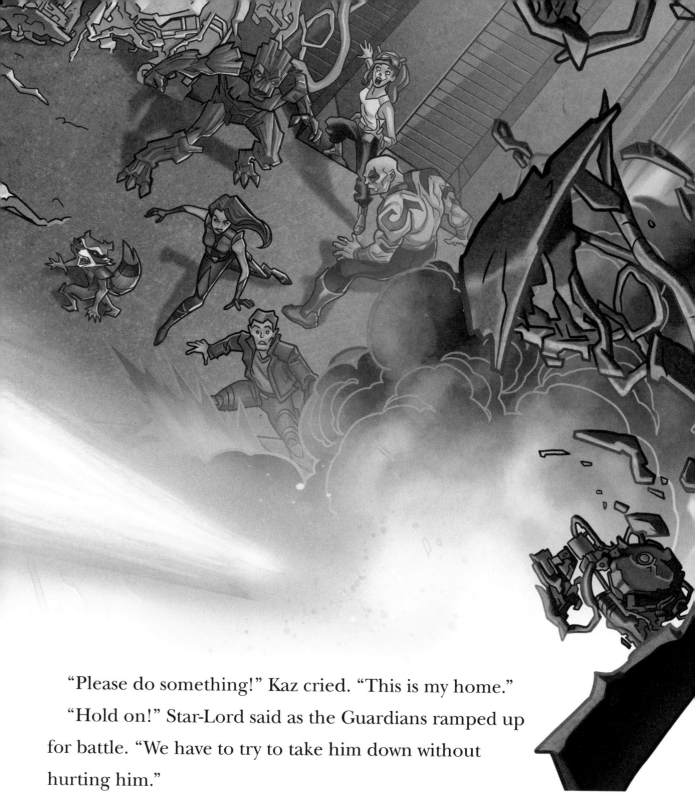

"Please do something!" Kaz cried. "This is my home."

"Hold on!" Star-Lord said as the Guardians ramped up for battle. "We have to try to take him down without hurting him."

"Agreed," Gamora said. "This isn't right. Iron Man wouldn't do something like this."

"Somebody should tell him that!" Rocket yelled as he and Groot jumped out of the way of a blast.

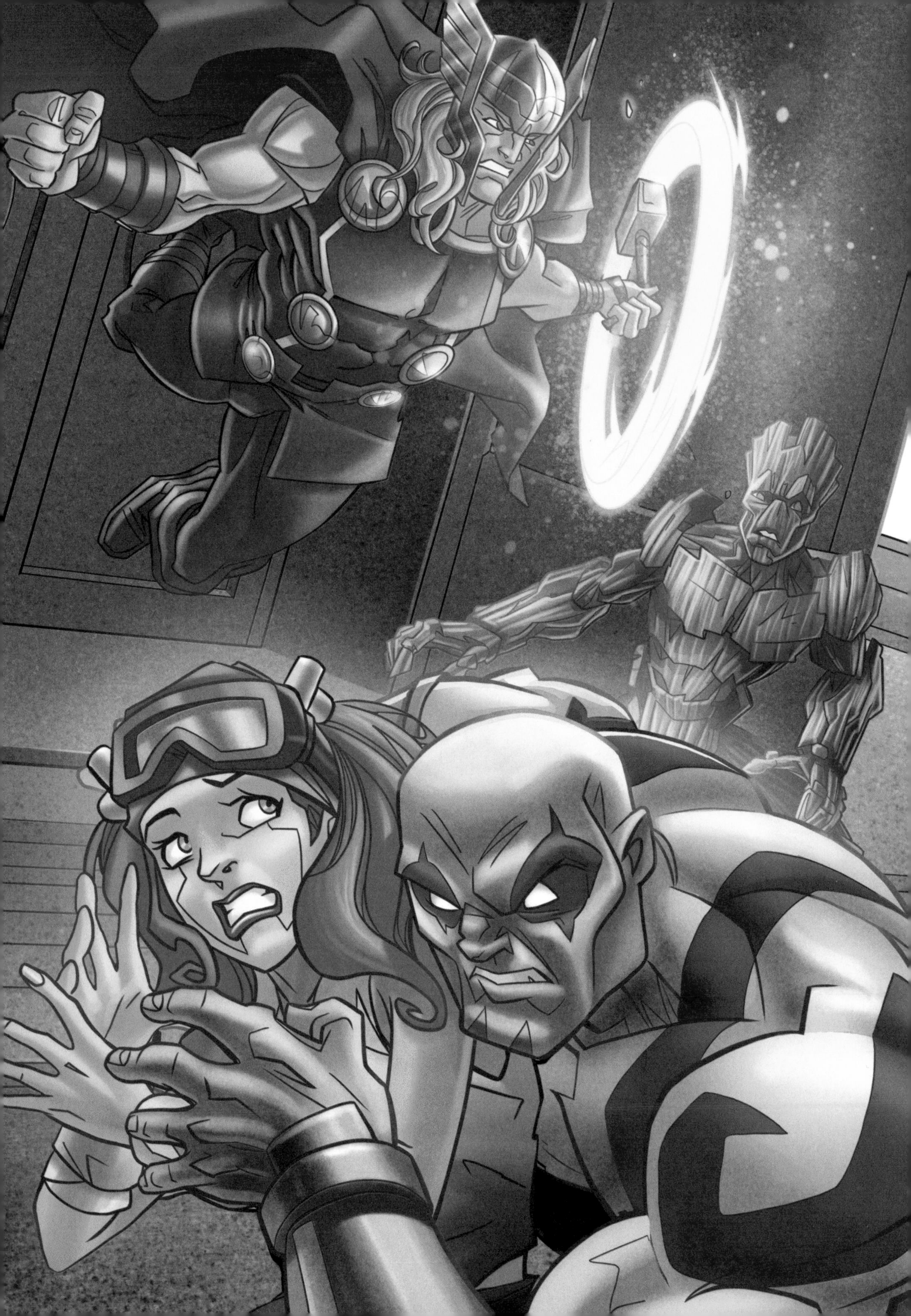

Suddenly a voice rang out overhead. "Need a hand?"

The Guardians looked up to see Thor, the Mighty Avenger!

"Wow, maybe I'm telepathic?" Rocket said, looking up at Thor in wonder.

"Or maybe I was on a mission to Xandar and heard the same distress signal you did," Thor replied.

"Speaking of which," Star-Lord said as he fired a blast at Iron Man, who easily maneuvered out of the way, "a little help, please?"

"Ah, yes," Thor said, focusing his attention on Iron Man, "this is highly unusual behavior."

"Well, what are you waiting for?" Rocket yelled, growing impatient with Thor's lack of urgency.

"You'll see," Thor said, "in three . . . two . . . NOW!"

At that moment, a green blur jumped out from a building behind Iron Man and slammed into the rampaging Avenger, knocking him to the ground.

"Hulk smash!"

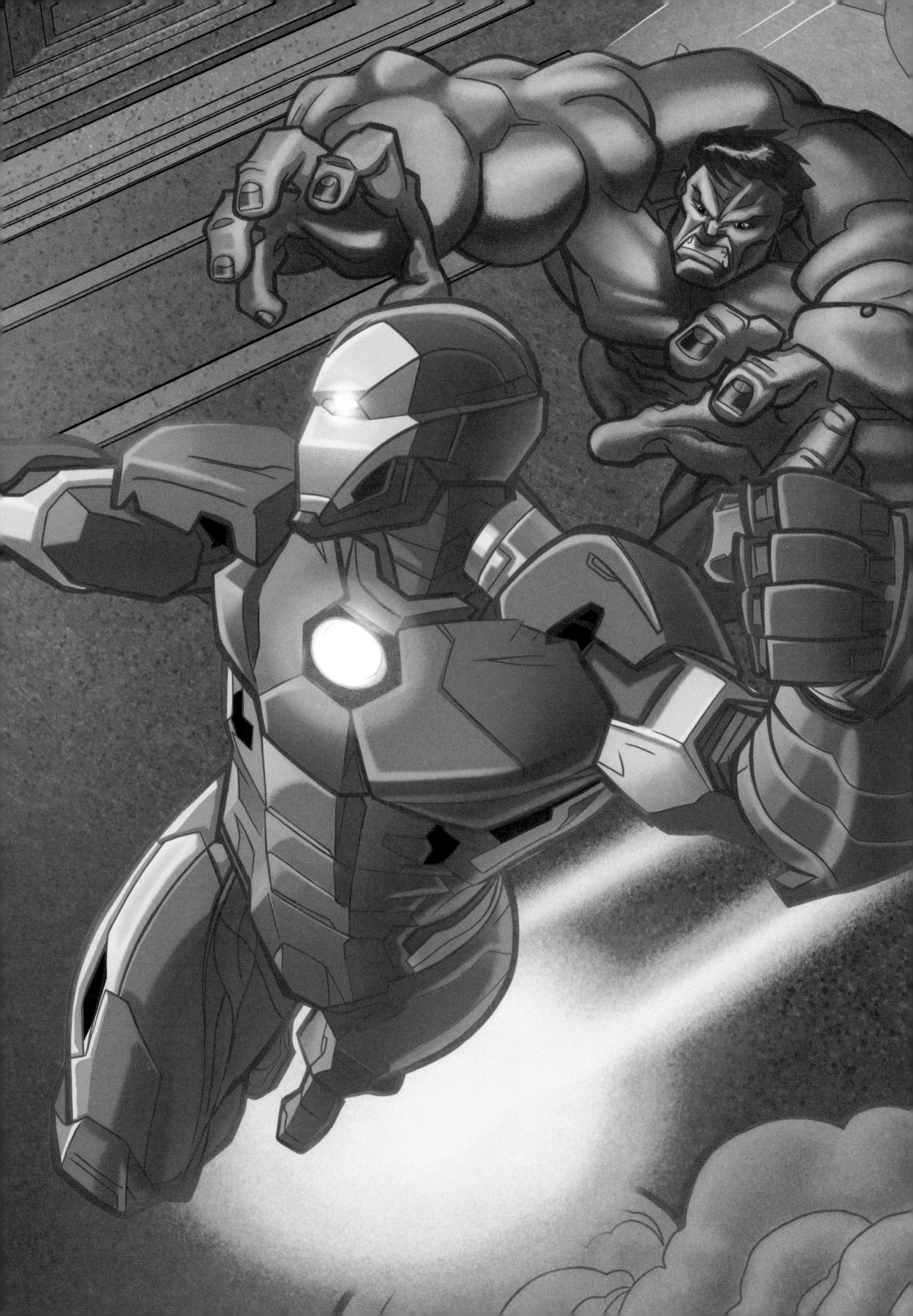

"I believe you know Hulk?" Thor said, landing on the ground where Hulk now had Iron Man pinned.

"I am Groot," Groot said.

"You're one to talk," Rocket replied. "You look pretty weird yourself."

Gamora nodded at Thor and Hulk. "Thanks for the assist, but what's gotten into Iron Man?"

"What's your plan here, huh?" Star-Lord said to Kaz, accusingly. "Is this some sort of big distraction?"

Kaz was shocked. "I . . . I don't know what you're talking about."

"Cut the act, sister," Star-Lord replied. "You're obviously behind this in some way."

Drax stepped in front of Kaz defensively. "What are you implying?" he asked Star-Lord.

"This is no coincidence," Star-Lord said. "Your girlfriend is totally evil!"

"Um, friends?" Thor said as he put his hand to his ear. He was receiving an urgent call through his communicator. "It's Tony Stark!"

"But if you're talking to Tony Stark, then who's that?" Gamora asked, pointing at the Iron Man suit on the ground.

"Only one way to find out," Star-Lord said, bending down to open Iron Man's helmet to find there was no one inside. "The suit is empty. But . . . it looks like his arc reactor has been tampered with!"

"Let me see it," Rocket said, examining the blinking gadget. "Hmm . . . I've seen these before. It's an ordinary tracking device. You can get them anywhere."

Gamora looked at Star-Lord, who was flustered. "I believe you owe Kaz an apology."

Star-Lord turned to Drax and Kaz. "Look, I'm sorry about earlier," he said. "I shouldn't have rushed to judgment."

"It's okay," Kaz said with a smile.

"We understand," Drax replied with a shrug. "You were just jealous."

Star-Lord groaned. "I am not jealous!"

Ultron Goes Viral

Alarm bells rang throughout Avengers Tower. Earth was in a state of emergency. Something horrific and unspeakable had happened. Something nobody should ever experience in their lifetime.

"The internet is down!" Iron Man shouted over the roar of the alarms. He had gathered the heroes on the roof of Avengers Tower.

Thor was confused. "So, humans can't watch their kitten videos?"

"All vital Earth systems need internet," Black Widow said grimly. "Hospitals, the electrical grid, you name it."

Captain America stepped forward, taking charge. "Hulk and Black Widow, check in with the police. Falcon, maintain the hospitals. Thor and Hawkeye, keep an eye out for trouble. Iron Man, you're with me. Let's go!"

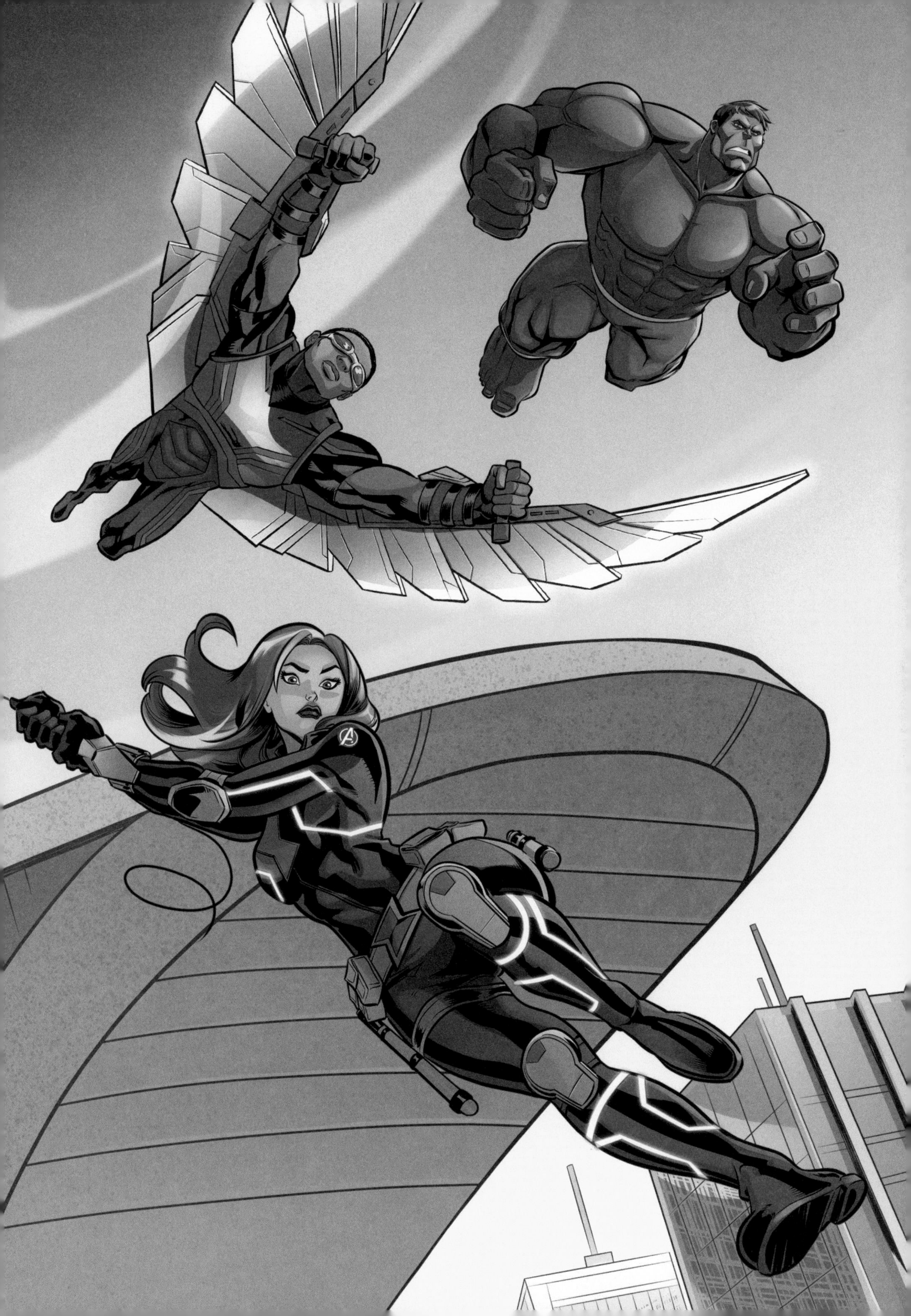

Captain America turned to Iron Man. "There has to be someone behind this."

"Way ahead of you, Cap," Iron Man replied. "JARVIS was able to do a deep dive into the world's servers. One name kept popping up. Ultron."

"The evil Artificial Intelligence?" Cap said, shaken.

Iron Man nodded. "I'm guessing he released a virus into the network. He wants to destroy everything. The question is, how do we destroy him?"

Captain America nodded. "I've got an idea."

With Iron Man using his rocket boots and Captain America on his sky-cycle, they headed toward their destination.

"I know you're a genius, Tony," Cap said, "but we need smarts and power. We need Captain Marvel."

"I've heard of her," Iron Man said. "What's her deal?"

"She's the head of Alpha Flight," Cap replied. "She's an astronaut, half-alien, and won't back down for anyone. Oh, and she lives in the Statue of Liberty's crown."

When they arrived they found Captain Marvel straightening her uniform. "Internet's down across the globe, and it's a complete mess," she said, not bothering to say hello first. "I assume that's why you boys are here?"

"Ultron released a virus," Iron Man explained, also not wasting words.

Captain Marvel nodded. She understood immediately. "I'm on it. Meet me at Alpha Flight Headquarters."

She grabbed her official Alpha Flight communicator. "Alpha Flight, prepare for my arrival." Captain Marvel then launched herself into the sky without even noticing Cap and Iron Man trying to catch up.

"How can her communicator be working?" Captain America asked as he and Iron Man tailed Captain Marvel.

"Alpha Flight must have bypassed the traditional network system, similar to JARVIS. I'm not surprised. Alpha Flight has some of the best tech around," Iron Man said. "Well, after Stark Industries, of course."

Cap smiled. "Of course."

Captain Marvel looked over her shoulder. "Come on, keep up!" The three heroes soared through the air and arrived at Alpha Flight Headquarters.

Alpha Flight gleamed with cutting-edge technology. Scientists, astronauts, engineers, and soldiers hurried to and fro.

Captain America and Iron Man watched in admiration as Captain Marvel strode into the room and immediately began issuing orders.

"Gonzalez!" she said. "Get an encrypted pipeline. O'Connell! Initiate offensive network protocol six-one-six."

Iron Man watched code scroll along the monitors. "It's digital warfare," he explained to Cap. "She's hunting Ultron's virus."

Soon everyone could see the plan was working. "Yes!" Captain Marvel yelled at her screen.

"Ultron is going to see where the threat is coming from," Iron Man warned her. "He'll come here to physically shut us down."

Captain Marvel smiled. "Let him come."

BOOM! Suddenly the wall behind Captain America exploded. Ultron appeared through the dust and mayhem. "Oh, how cute," he said. "Iron Man and Captain America think they can foil my genius plot to destroy human civilization."

Ultron grabbed Cap's shield, catching him off guard. But the hero wasn't about to give up so easily. "Bad idea, buddy."

Ultron just laughed as Captain America leaped into action. He flung his shield at Ultron and hit him with a powerful punch. But Ultron was too strong. He grabbed Captain America and threw him out of the building through the massive hole in the wall!

Cap dangled off the side of the building as Ultron turned to Iron Man and the Alpha Flight team. "Give up, puny humans. Your Earth systems don't stand a chance. Nobody can protect humanity now!"

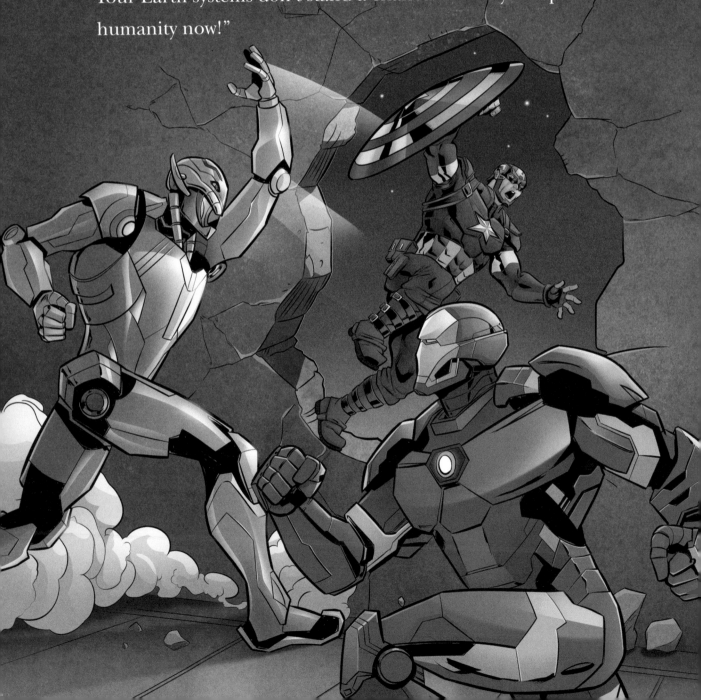

It was a fearsome speech, but suddenly Iron Man began to laugh. "You've never met Captain Marvel, have you?"

Ultron sneered, looking at Captain Marvel. "This human woman and her pathetic little friends? I will destroy them!"

Captain Marvel glared at Ultron. Then, tightening her gloves, she nodded at her first lieutenant.

"I'm only half-human," Captain Marvel said as the lieutenant hit the button that said EXECUTE.

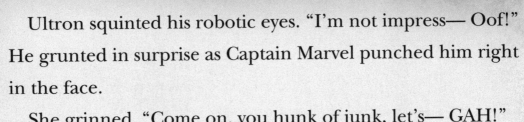

Ultron squinted his robotic eyes. "I'm not impress— Oof!" He grunted in surprise as Captain Marvel punched him right in the face.

She grinned. "Come on, you hunk of junk, let's— GAH!"

Ultron tackled her to the ground with a *CRASH!* Their fight raged all over Alpha Flight Headquarters as everyone scrambled for cover. Before long, both were bruised and battered. One of Captain Marvel's strongest punches had put a big dent in Ultron's cheek!

"This is getting boring," Captain Marvel said. "And since our code is nearly done executing . . ."

BING! the computer announced.

"There we go," Captain Marvel said, smiling sweetly. "Your virus is toast, Ultron. And so are you."

Captain Marvel swung a mighty punch. The blow was so powerful that Ultron burst through the wall and sailed straight into space!

"What'd I miss?" Captain America asked as he made his way back up to Headquarters. Captain Marvel and Iron Man looked at each other and burst out laughing. Tony had to take off his helmet in order to catch his breath.

"Up high," Tony said, raising a hand.

"The internet's back up," she said, high-fiving Tony, "and Ultron is out of our hair. Great work today, heroes!"

Tony smiled. "Sorry, Steve, but it looks like the Avengers have a new captain now."